ASSASSIN'S TOUCH

IRON PORTAL #1

Laurie London

LB Books
Seattle, Washington

Cover art/design: Patricia Schmitt (Pickyme)
Cover photography: Jenn LeBlanc

Laurie London/LB Books
Seattle, WA

Publisher's Note: This is a work of fiction. Names, characters, places, and incidents are a product of the author's imagination. Locales and public names are sometimes used for atmospheric purposes. Any resemblance to actual people, living or dead, or to businesses, companies, events, institutions, or locales is completely coincidental.

Book Layout ©2013 BookDesignTemplates.com

Assassin's Touch/ Laurie London. -- 1st ed.
ISBN: 978-1507705438

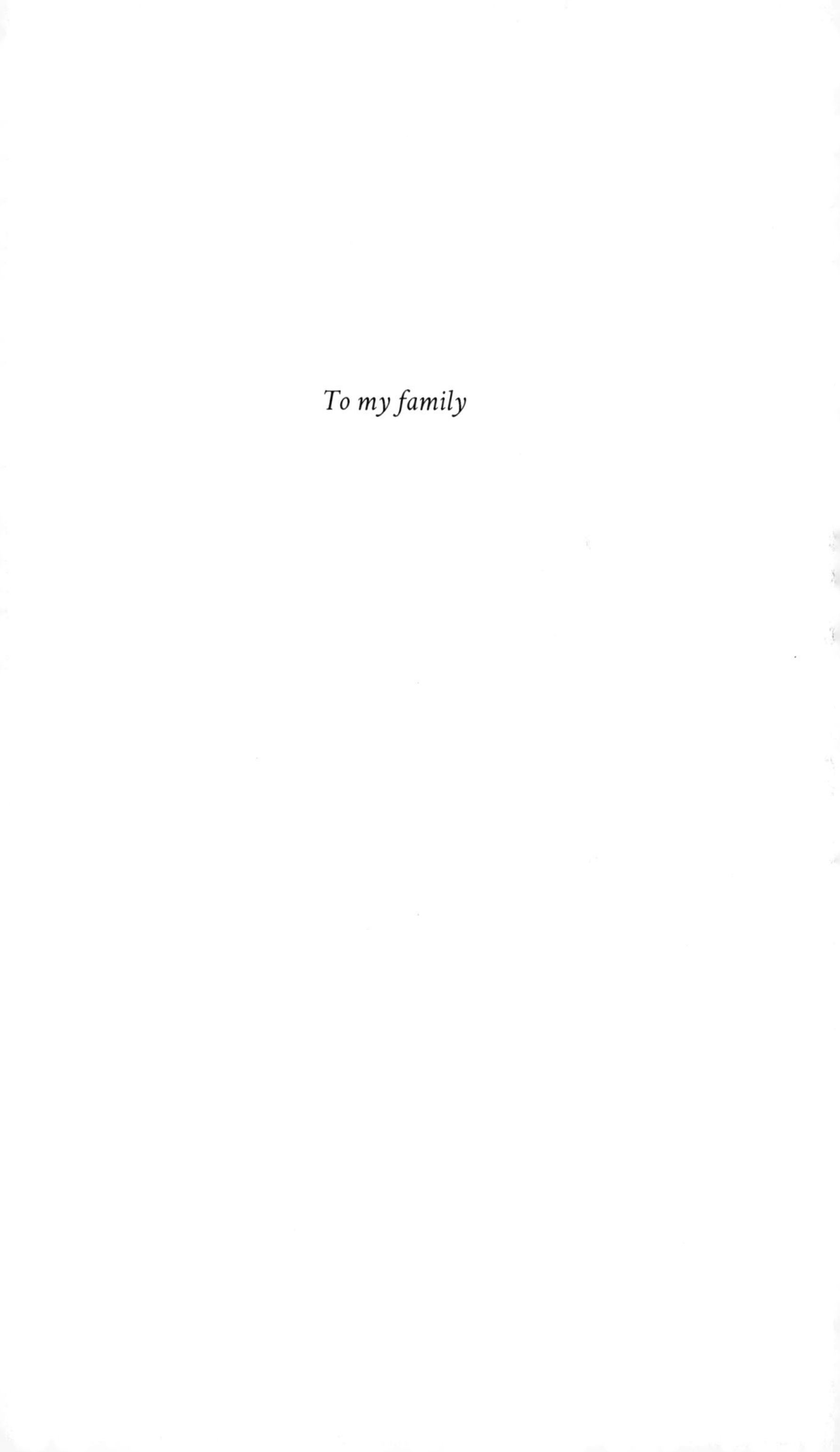

To my family

CHAPTER ONE

"Agent Trihorn!"

Neyla jumped to her feet, stashing the book on the seat behind her. With her heart pounding in her chest, she steeled her shoulders and saluted.

Where had Captain Gravich come from? Last she knew, he was two railcars away lecturing the recruits fresh from boot camp about the origins of the current conflict. Having endured that talk before, she assumed he'd be busy until they arrived at the station. She was such a fool for sneaking out her paperback.

He stormed down the aisle, his irritation souring the already stale air like pungent body odor. The other soldiers in the car subtly moved away from her. She couldn't blame them. No doubt they were thinking it was better that *she* took the brunt of their captain's ire, not them.

Sweat formed on her upper lip as he stopped just to her left, but she didn't dare wipe it off. With eyes forward, she stood at attention, preparing for the onslaught.

"What the hell do you think you're doing?" He leaned in much too close—he'd had onions for breakfast. "We're pulling into the Crystal Peak station in three minutes, but you're obviously distracted and not ready. Where's your damn head, Trihorn?"

They were that close? God, the book had totally sucked her in, whisking her to a fictional world very different from her own. Although it did a good job of keeping her mind off things she didn't want to think about, she was mad at herself for not being able to multitask a little better. She should've been paying attention to what was going on around her.

"I'm sorry, sir. I won't let it happen again."

Out of the corner of her eye, she saw him tap a meaty finger to his temple. "If I didn't know you better, Trihorn, I'd think your heart wasn't in this mission."

"It is, sir."

"I'm not so sure. You're obviously unfocused and easily distracted. To be successful, you've got to feel it here." He pounded a fist against his barrel chest, reminding her of a plump, preening bird. "You need to be passionate about what you do. Live it, breathe it. Focus on it at all times rather than on this—" He picked up her book and scowled. "—drivel. Otherwise, defeat and failure will follow you everywhere."

"Amen."

"Bravo."

She tried to ignore the bootlickers. "It's just that..."

But she couldn't tell him why—especially not in front

of everyone. Her fellow soldiers zeroed in on any sign of weakness like a pack of feral dogs, even one of their own. Plus, the fact that she'd received a direct commission as an officer and skipped the rigorous basic training hadn't sat well with a few of them. She didn't need to give them more fodder.

"I am ready, sir." Just then, the rail car jerked and she almost choked. Through some miracle, she managed to keep her balance without clutching at the overhead handle like a terrified idiot.

Rather than tossing the book aside, Captain Gravich began to thumb through the pages. She kicked herself for daring to read a physical book. If she'd been reading an electronic version on her handheld, he'd have assumed she was working.

"Well, look at this. An I-love-you-truly book."

Someone laughed.

Oh great. This wasn't going to be pleasant. If only she could melt into the seat behind her. She hated confrontation and had never been good at thinking on her feet anyway. The perfect thing to say always came five minutes or an hour after the fact, when she'd had plenty of time to mull things over.

"Yes, sir," she said simply. She didn't need to justify her reading choices to him. If she did say something, it'd probably sound stupid and defensive.

"Does it help you concentrate, Agent Trihorn?" The

derision in his tone was obvious.

She heard another snicker. What really made her cringe, though, was seeing Captain Gravich creasing the cover. She wanted to grab it out of his hands as if he were a child touching something he shouldn't. She never bent her books that way. When she finished reading them, they still looked brand new.

"Does it get you into the right frame of mind for this mission?"

Guess reading a book filled with serial killers, heads on spikes, or unhappy people searching for inner peace would be more acceptable.

Hoping this public humiliation would be over soon, she sucked up her pride. "I...I enjoy reading on the train, sir. I'm sorry. It won't happen again."

His onion breath flitted across her cheek once. Twice.

She stood her ground, looking straight ahead. How could she tell him that ever since the wreck last year—the one that had changed everything—she was terrified of anything that remotely reminded her of the inside of a train? When forced to ride in one, she did whatever she could to keep her mind elsewhere. Reading, doing crossword puzzles, using her favorite sketching app on her handheld. She used to listen to music, but given what had happened the last time she'd had earbuds in, she'd vowed not to make that mistake again.

"Well, then, step lively," he said finally, tossing the book down. "Our latest intel shows the portal might be closer than we thought. No doubt their men are guarding it carefully and will be waiting for us. We need your abilities as a Talent more than ever to have any hope of finding it and defeating the barbarians. They bombed another nightclub in New Seattle last night. Did you know that?"

She tried not to appear too relieved that his interrogation was over. "Yes, sir. That's terrible, sir."

It was all over the army news blogs. She'd seen the photos and videos of the destruction when she logged in this morning. Heaps of dusty red bricks littered the sidewalks, and blown-out windows gaped as dark as a devil's mouth.

One image, that of a young woman in tattered clothes and clutching a high-heeled shoe, stuck with her. Except for the brown hair, it could easily have been herself last year. Confused. Scared. Not sure why she was alive when so many others hadn't been so lucky. She'd spent hours in the small hospital bathroom, trying to get the scent of burning flesh off her skin and out of her hair. As the days turned into months, she kept expecting the nightmares would fade, but so far, they hadn't. Her memories were as vivid as ever.

Neyla shivered and gave in to her need to fidget. Trying not to be too obvious, she bit the inside of her cheek and tapped her toes inside her boot. At least the Captain valued her as a Talent. That should count for something.

"We're going to find the bastards and bring them to justice." With a grunt of dismissal, he finally stomped down the aisle.

Thank God. He could make her life unbearable if he wanted to. From now on, she needed to do a better job of keeping her head in the game so crap like this wouldn't happen. She tucked the book into her duffel, and when the doors of the train slid open, she shuffled onto the platform along with the other members of her unit.

"If you slow us down on this mission like you did before, Trihorn, I'll make sure it's your last." Although the voice hissed from behind, she knew it was Corporal Smythe. His buddies called him The Snake. Very fitting, if you asked her. She hated reptiles.

"Promise?" She tried to disguise the word with a cough. In the time she'd been with the Special Tactics and Response Team, she'd grown tired of violence junkies like Smythe. Even if they did fight against vicious warriors from the Barrowlands, it didn't make the situation any easier. Before her special abilities were discovered, the closest she'd come to warfare was sitting in front of her flat screen playing online video games with her brother.

The Captain's lecture about passion still echoed in her head, serving as a painful reminder of everything she'd lost.

When the army ordered her to join the ranks as a Talent—though they preferred to call it an *invitation*—she was forced to sell her costume design boutique. She had nothing to return to now. Her customers had moved on. Her cute little shop, with its shabby chic décor, was now a coffee house. It was as if her former self had never existed.

For the thousandth time, she cursed those warmongering barbarians for putting her in this situation in the first place. If they hadn't slipped through their secret portals from the Barrowlands to bring death and destruction to her world, she wouldn't be here, enduring life rather than living it. Without the train wreck, her Talent may have remained latent. And if not, it would simply have been a parlor trick, a silly game to pull on friends during happy hour at the Dungeness & Dragons Pub.

At least her father had been proud of her before he'd passed away, and for that she was grateful. He'd said he always knew she had a Talent in her. That she was finally doing something worthwhile instead of wasting time making silly clothes for rich people to play dress-up.

Shifting the duffel strap to the other shoulder as the

platform filled up around her, she refocused her thoughts away from her own discomfort. She couldn't forget that her special ability had prevented a lot of suffering—and deaths. She needed to see the bigger picture, to be woman enough to do what was right, not just what was easy or comfortable.

"We don't need you." Smythe jammed an elbow in her back, causing her to stumble into another soldier.

"What an ass," she murmured.

"Excuse me?" The guy in front of her turned around.

Her cheeks heated with embarrassment. "Sorry. Not you."

"No worries," he said, smiling. "The place is packed."

Though she didn't recognize him, she did notice the thin, pale line of skin along his hairline. New military haircut equaled new recruit. And here she was starting off on the wrong foot with him.

His glance darted to the Talent insignia affixed to her uniform. Though it was subtle, his upper lip puckered slightly, as if he'd bit into a lemon, and his eyes narrowed. Without waiting for her to say anything more, he turned around, leaving her to stare at his backpack.

Even the START newbies welcomed her presence like a leper in a nursery. It was like they taught this stuff at boot camp.

Wishing she wasn't the only Talent on this mission,

she stood on her tiptoes to scan the crowd for the twins, Jaden and Justina. Their bright red hair would be hard to miss. But since most of the soldiers were a good head taller, she wasn't able to see much.

She shifted her weight from one foot to the other and waited for Captain Gravich to address them. Soon they would be loaded into the transport vehicles and taken into the forest surrounding Crystal Peak. Unless he'd changed the latest plans, she'd be stationed behind her individual unit, the Fighting Red Wolves. This time, they were fairly removed from the front lines, which was good. Being in the field with the rest of the R-Dubs hadn't exactly worked out well on their last mission.

"We've never needed your *Talent,*" Smythe whispered, his voice barely loud enough to be heard over the din.

Not again. "Why don't you just crawl away, Corporal, and stop bugging me?" And even though she shouldn't, she added, "Somewhere, there's a rock missing you."

He sucked in a breath through his teeth. Good. She'd pissed him off.

From day one, she'd endured his nasty comments and his grade-school-bully pranks. Given what had just happened with Gravich, she really wasn't in the mood to deal with him now.

"You're dead weight, Trihorn. We're better and

faster without you."

She wanted to tell him to take it up with their superiors—they were the ones who insisted she be a part of the unit—but she kept her mouth shut. She'd baited Corporal Smythe enough already.

* * *

The rock formation felt cold and slightly damp as Rickert D'Angelus flattened himself against the side of Crystal Peak. He stood on a wide ledge just beneath the top of the cliff with a rain-swollen river raging hundreds of feet below. Low voices murmured in the darkness—at least three or four Pacifica soldiers. With the Iron Portal no more than a furlong away, the enemy was too close. He'd have to take them out here.

Silently, he drew his blade and held it between his teeth. He found a toehold, but as he began to pull himself up, a warm sensation flitted across the skin of his forearms and he stepped back onto the ledge.

Damn. A Talent.

How could he have been so foolish as to not check for one of their army's rare para-ability soldiers before he got this close? Even though it had been months since he'd encountered a Talent on this side of the portal, it was inexcusable for a Warrior of the Iron Guild to make a mistake of this magnitude. A mistake that could cost not only his life, but the lives of his men scattered throughout the area.

Not daring to breathe, he hoped the bloke wasn't a Telepathy-Talent or a Psychic-Talent. He'd sense Rickert for sure. When he realized the idiocy of that thought, he allowed himself a grim smile. If their Talent could read minds or see the future, Rickert would already be dead.

With his body pressed against the rock wall, he wondered what tricks they were up to. Usually they kept those with para-abilities back with the commanding officer while the regular men did the fighting. They were too valuable to risk out in the field.

And then the reason occurred to him.

The portal.

Of course.

He glanced in the direction of the hidden entrance halfway down the cliff face. The Pacificans had to know it was nearby, and were using this Talent to pinpoint the exact location. Finding it must be worth that risk.

Footsteps crunched on the path above him. Two soldiers had left, but by his estimate, two others remained. Rickert couldn't pull himself up to the top and kill them quite yet. Not until he knew they were retreating. At that point, he'd slip silently behind them and slit their throats. They'd be dead before they hit the ground.

"Hey!" A man's voice rang out—so close that Rickert considered grabbing the bloke's ankle and sending him plummeting to his death.

But if he did, the second soldier might have just enough time to sound an alarm, alerting others before Rickert could climb the rest of the way up and get to him. No, he'd wait as long as it took, then kill them both.

"Me and the guys are tired of you slowing us down," the man was saying to the other soldier.

Although he couldn't be sure, Rickert didn't think the one speaking had para-abilities—the night air would've felt faintly charged when the guy spoke. Not all of his people could sense someone with Talents the way Rickert could, which was one of the reasons he was in charge. That and the fact that he was the group's most lethal assassin. Revenge made him take personal risks that no one else would. Or should. He would never order his men to do the things he did. A few of them had families back home, while he, on the other hand, had nothing to lose.

"The R-Dubs lost the A-1 ranking because of you."

"I admit that was my fault, but you think I had a choice?" At the sound of the woman's voice, a subtle tingle skated over Rickert's arms.

Bloody hell, their Talent was female? He hadn't been expecting that.

She continued, but this time her voice took on a

ragged edge. "Do you honestly think I enjoy stretching out my mental senses to shield you from harm? I can think of a million other things I'd rather do, but you lived, didn't you? That should count for something."

"Danger is something we live with—mediocrity isn't. And given our status as the best fighting unit in START, your talents are unnecessary. We don't need your *protection.*"

Rickert heard a scuffle and a few tiny rocks skittered over his head.

"Smythe, don't."

The metallic sound of a blade being unsheathed cut through the quiet night air, and the man grunted. "Damn you. Why won't this work?"

"Because I'm a Protection-Talent, that's why. When I see Captain Gravich, I'm going to file a formal complaint against you this time and— Wait! Wait!"

Rickert heard the sound of boots above him.

"Oh, please don't."

More rocks fell from the edge, followed by a dark shape. It narrowly missed Rickert and landed with a thud near his feet. The woman moaned and rolled to her side.

What the bloody hell was going on? Weren't these two fighting for the same side?

"Oh, for chrissake," the man muttered. "That bitch's got nine lives." From the sound of it, he was leaning over the edge.

Every muscle in Rickert's body froze. He didn't dare breathe. He prayed to the Fates that he was hidden enough in the shadows. If the guy spotted him—

The soldier cursed again and landed on the ledge with a grunt. Rickert smiled to himself. It wasn't often that the enemy fell into his lap like this. First the woman, then the man. He'd make quick work of these two, then meet up with the others at the rendezvous point.

With his arms held slightly away from his body, as if they were too muscular to hang straight down, the pale-haired bloke strutted toward the woman. Enemy differences aside, he had an air about him that made Rickert want to plunge a knife into his belly just for the hell of it.

Palming his blade, he'd strike in three, two, one—

"Let's see if you can survive this," the man said, and kicked the woman.

Mo naire! What the bloody fuck was that?

Drawing her knees into a fetal position, the female soldier made no move to fight back or defend herself.

What kind of soldier would turn on one of his own—especially a woman who sure as hell didn't act like a soldier?

Ha! The kind of soldier who just took his last breath.

Before the man could kick her again, Rickert slipped

from the shadows. In one silent movement, he grasped a handful of the man's hair, drew a blade across his throat, and the soldier slid to the ground as if his ligaments had turned to gel.

Rickert kicked the body over the edge and watched as it fell hundreds of feet to land at awkward angles on the river rocks below. He turned back to the woman. Of average height and with blond hair covering her face, she wore camouflage army fatigues and black boots. A Protection-Talent, huh? Then she probably wasn't seriously injured.

Now what? It wasn't like he could leave her to attract the attention of the other soldiers, especially not this close to the entrance. He rubbed a hand absently over his arm before realizing that the leather-corded necklace he kept wrapped around his wrist was on the other side of the portal. Twisting his blade, he watched the moonlight flash its reflection in the cold-forged Balkirk steel.

Why had one of her own tried to kill her? What had she done to deserve that? Recalling the brutal attack invading Pacificans had made on his family's village a few years ago, he wasn't surprised that these people were capable of senseless violence. No matter how long he lived, he'd never forget what awaited him in Summer's Folly when he returned late one night. Violence between fighting men was one thing, but against innocent villagers...his own flesh and blood....

Anger pulsed through his veins like the river raging below him, feeding his never-ending quest for revenge.

Bloody hell, he hated them. Every single damn one of them. Including this woman.

Three quick whistle bursts, like the screech of a night bat, pierced the air. It was Asher, his second in command.

Given that she was a Protection-Talent, the dagger probably wouldn't work on her anyway. Besides, he didn't want to damage it to find out—the sturdy blade was one of his favorites. He'd been iron sick for days after bringing it through the portal, and didn't relish the thought of suffering through that again just to get a new one. After tucking the weapon into the leather sheath strapped to his back, he whistled a sharp reply to Asher. Maybe they could figure out how to use her Talent to their advantage.

He bent over, planning to drag her away from the edge, but she weighed so little that he ended up hoisting her into his arms instead. One of her hands wedged against his torso, cold against his bare skin. As he straightened, a misty haze filled his vision. He stumbled and fell to his knees, careful not to drop her.

He blinked a few times, thinking he'd stood too quickly, but the mist before him remained. The cloud began to swirl and dissipate somewhat, revealing a figure in the center.

No, two people. A man and a woman. They were...

They were making love.

Rickert sat back hard on his haunches, the soldier still cradled in his arms.

The woman in the mist skimmed her hands down the man's back, over the crest of his hip, digging her nails to urge him deeper. The man's ass flexed as he drove into her with long, powerful thrusts.

Their movements became more frenzied until suddenly the man stopped, buried all the way to the hilt. He arched his back and—

Holy bollocks! They were climaxing together.

Rickert scrubbed a hand over his face as his cock swelled in automatic response to this erotic imagery playing out before him, even though it...couldn't be real.

The two stayed joined for a moment—the man cradled between her bent knees, the woman gently caressing his back—before he finally rolled off. Rickert couldn't hear them, but he imagined they were whispering words of love to each other.

The man kissed her tenderly in response to something she said, and placed a broad hand on her belly, filling the space from hipbone to hipbone. And as he did so, a strange yet pleasurable sensation roiled through Rickert's body. Different from the easily sated lust he was accustomed to, this was something deeper, more emotional.

Through the years he'd bedded many women, but he'd never made love to any of them as this man made love to this woman. With such passion and significance. Was this what it felt like to love and be loved back? To have a future filled with the promise of such happiness?

He didn't know, because he'd never thought about these things for himself. Protecting his people and preventing the deaths of innocents were his only priorities. When his sister had died so brutally at the hands of the enemy, he vowed to focus on nothing else. It'd be pure selfishness to think otherwise.

A sharp realization filled his mind, like a drop of water that sizzles when it's flicked onto a hot skillet. The woman was about to conceive the man's child from this lovemaking. At this very moment, the man's seed was inside her, searching for its target, and her body was waiting to meet it. Although how or why Rickert knew this, he didn't have a clue, but he was absolutely certain.

Rickert exhaled slowly, letting a quiet calmness fall over him. *Shhh,* he wanted to whisper to them. *Be still. Let the Fates work their magic.*

As the couple slept blissfully in each other's arms, the mist thinned out further, and the faces came into focus. The man's dark, wavy hair fell to his shoulders and the familiar face, which had always seemed angry when it stared at Rickert from a mirror, now looked peaceful and content.

"Bloody hell!"

No. Impossible. It couldn't be.

He pushed the woman away and dragged himself to his feet, the mist disappearing into the cool night air. He tried to inhale deeply, but all he could manage were a few strangled breaths.

He was that man.

And the beautiful woman—the one from the mist—was the hurt little soldier before him.

CHAPTER TWO

"I say we kick her over the edge," Asher said as his dog sniffed the woman's foot. Even though Conry often trotted ahead, scouting independently, the deerhound was never far from the man. The two were inseparable...in both worlds. "It's got to be two hundred feet down to the river and Snoqualmie Falls isn't far away. No one can survive going over that."

The sour sting of bile rose in Rickert's throat at the thought of harm coming to the woman, but he wasn't about to tell his second in command what he'd seen in his head. Asher would simply say the vision was Talent trickery at work.

A *seun,* a spell.

Or maybe just the muddled mind of a desperate man.

Before each mission, Rickert took a vow of celibacy in order to channel all available energy into killing the enemy. Asher always thought that was bullshit, and never passed up an opportunity to dally under the skirts in either realm.

"We can't take the chance she'd live and join up with another unit," Rickert said. "Protection-Talents are extremely rare and almost impossible to kill. Their army would waste no time putting her into action again before our mission here is complete."

The other man started to protest, but Rickert cut him off. "Besides, they're getting close to the Crestenfahl portal. We can't make it any easier for them by letting her go back."

Asher brushed away a thin black braid that had slipped from its tie. Considering his tight-fitting T-shirt and ripped jeans, he'd clearly stolen the clothes from someone who didn't give a damn about his appearance. The only place they belonged was in a fire pit, but that was just Rickert's opinion. His men were free to make their own choices, even if they wanted to look like New Seattle street thugs.

He rubbed a hand over his worn leather kilt. Practical and easy. What a proud Iron Guild warrior *should* wear.

"So what are you proposing we do if you don't want to kill her?" Asher asked.

"Take her prisoner and see what kind of information we can extract."

Asher frowned as if Rickert had just smoked an entire bowl of *prath* in one of the Crestenfahl hookah pubs, and was now trying to carry on an intelligent conversation. "Through the portal? We haven't taken a prisoner in... Damn, I can't even remember the last time."

"True, but we've never captured a Talent before,

either."

"But there are families there, Rickert," Asher said through clenched teeth. "Babies."

"She's not a threat."

"You know that for sure?"

"Yes," he said icily.

"And who do you think can take her through?" Asher patted Conry's wiry gray coat. "Most of the men just came over and won't be able to make another crossing for a few weeks."

His friend was right. No one would risk being violently ill for days. Portal sickness was much worse than being seasick. And if done too often, a crossing could be deadly.

An explosion sounded from the other side of the canyon. The woman stirred, but still didn't wake. Even unconscious, she made a lousy soldier.

"I'll take her." The moment the words tumbled out, Rickert felt himself relax...and he knew instantly this was the right thing to do.

"Are you crazy? We need you here. What about the munitions bunker? Who's going to set the charges?"

"Toryn and Konal. They're just as capable as I am. And you know the locations of the explosives caches. Besides, you said so yourself—there's no one else to take her through." He glanced at the position of the stars. "Daybreak is coming. We both must leave."

"But...you've got more kills than the rest of us combined."

Rickert cursed. Since when had his authority turned into a democracy? Maybe Asher had been spending too much time here and had forgotten how things worked back home.

"Enough. My decision is final."

* * *

"Let's go."

Something hard jabbed Neyla's upper arm. Her head pounded like a lopsided jackhammer, the ground was gritty sandpaper against her cheek. There was a muted stillness to the air, suggesting she wasn't in the forest.

"Come on. Get up." A man's voice and that annoying poking again. A boot. Probably with a steel toe, given how hard it felt against her arm.

Wait—the cliff.

"Get away from me, Smythe." She held up her hands, feeling vulnerable and angry all over again. But the moment she spoke, she realized it wasn't his voice she'd heard.

"I'm not Smythe."

The accent sounded—strange. One of the new guys? She probably should've introduced herself to the recruits, but given what had happened at the train, she'd been reluctant to reach out to any of them.

What mattered most right now was having this guy help her get back to the command post. She'd tell the Captain what Smythe had done, then take some heavy duty Tylenol, find the empty bunk where she'd stashed her duffel, and go to sleep.

"On your feet. Hurry."

Jeez, whoever this was, he sure was bossy. He couldn't be a friend of Smythe's, could he? God, she hoped not. She cupped her forehead, trying to contain the pounding inside.

Resigning herself to the fact that she couldn't just lie here, that she needed to actually get up, she sighed and rolled over. A quick glance revealed she was just inside the mouth of a cave. A large shadow of a man with his legs spread, hands on his hips, stood at her feet. With the night sky behind him, she couldn't make out any details other than his formidable size.

"What unit are you from? Where am I?" Neyla pushed herself to her feet while he just stood there and didn't offer to help. He kept his hands tucked into his—

She saw a slight movement of cloth near his hips. Was that a loincloth? A *kilt*?

Panic roared in her ears and her focus narrowed like an arrow speeding toward its target.

An assassin from the Barrowlands.

She reached for her gun. It was gone. The knife at

her hip—gone. She sidestepped him, jumped toward the front of the cave, but he drew a large sword and blocked her path.

The throbbing in her head intensified. She pressed the heels of her hands against her eyebrows and couldn't help staggering backward.

What should she do? What *could* she do? What was army protocol in situations like this?

God, she had absolutely no idea.

* * *

The air cooled with each step as Rickert marched his prisoner deeper into the cavern. The woman stumbled again.

"Pick your feet up and you won't trip so much."

"I can't see. Don't you have a flashlight?"

"No," he growled, not bothering to hide his exasperation. Bloody hell. He could walk faster with his eyes closed.

If he could throw her over his shoulder, it'd make things much easier, but he didn't dare give her the chance to plant another hallucination, especially now that she was awake. The first vision on the ledge could simply have been an anomaly, but it had happened again as he'd carried the unconscious woman to the portal entrance. And, of course, it had to be another one of those damn sex fantasies.

A Talent trick, maybe—an instinctual protection technique activated by physical touch to keep an enemy from harming her. It was brilliant, actually, getting your enemy to sympathize with you. After seeing and feeling *that,* he wasn't exactly compelled to draw his blade across the throat of his dream lover. Not that it'd even work, given her Talent, but he sure as hell wasn't going to let himself dwell on what he'd seen in those visions. She was his prisoner—nothing more.

If he wanted them to speed things up beyond this snail's pace, he'd have to light a couple of wall torches, which didn't really appeal to him. He preferred to stay secret and anonymous on this side of the portal, living in the darkness and shadows. No one over here who saw him as a Cascadian assassin lived to tell anyone about it. But what was the point? She'd see him when they got to the other side anyway.

She tripped again, almost falling to her knees. *Och.* At this rate, it'd take them another hour to get there. With a slight nod of his head, he concentrated on a wall torch up ahead. It fizzled and sparked before bursting into flames. She gasped and stopped in her tracks, her hands flying up to shield her eyes. He almost ran into her.

"What...magic is this? How did you—"

The little hairs on his arm tickled when she spoke, and he rubbed the sensation away. Figures a Pacifican soldier would think such a thing. Magic had been gone a long time, used up centuries ago during the Obsidian Wars, when the worlds had been divided. However, her people were convinced his side still had reserves hidden away and were desperate to get at them. "No magic, soldier, just Talent."

He wasn't as powerful as she was—his only ability was a weak command over fire, which wasn't even strong enough to be considered a Fire-Talent—but he certainly wasn't going to tell her that. Let her think he could do all sorts of things.

Her eyes widened. "You're a Talent, too?" Her lyrical voice contrasted with the harsh accent of a Pacifican to make a most captivating combination. Like sweet and sour. Being able to see once again had definitely given her courage.

He allowed himself to examine her a little more closely. She was petite, at least a head shorter than he was, and fine-boned. In the torchlight, her golden hair shimmered, and he found himself wondering how it'd feel between his fingers. Would the strands glide through like silk? Her almond-shaped eyes were the color of emeralds flecked with tiny bits of gold that reflected the light. Praise the Fates, even in this shapeless army uniform, she was beautiful.

One brow arched quizzically upward, as if she were waiting for him to do something. "If you're not going to answer, then at least tell me where you're taking me."

That snapped him out of the spell. Enough of this nonsense. A celibate warrior didn't let himself get side-tracked like this. Even by an incredibly gorgeous woman.

"To a jail pit in Cascadia."

She took a step back, her gaze darting left and right. "You're taking me into the Barrowlands? The portal is here?"

He bristled at that term. It implied that his world was on the fringe, created as an afterthought to her steel and concrete world, rather than the other way around. "Where did you think I was taking you? To one of your shopping malls?"

"You're a—a barbarian."

She was calling *him* a barbarian? The irony made him laugh. No use arguing—she'd find out soon enough. Their jail pits weren't exactly civilized.

Her nostrils flared as she scrutinized him from head to toe like a piece of meat, her gaze leaving a trail of sparks over his skin. He was mildly surprised when his cock stirred again between his legs, brushing against the leather kilt. He'd always been attracted to strong, confident women, but clearly, his already poor judgment had been unduly influenced by those tantalizing visions. His vow of celibacy notwithstanding, he was normally much stronger than this.

He fingered the hilt of his sword to remind himself of who he was—and that she was his bloody enemy. "Go," he said gruffly.

She didn't budge. "Release me at once."

This petite thing was giving him orders? He choked back another laugh. "You got full of fire once you laid eyes on me," he said, holding his arms straight out from his sides. "I must look like a fool or buffoon and not the fighting man I thought I was."

"If you let me go, I promise not to say anything. I have a terrible sense of direction—I'd never be able to find this place again."

She couldn't be serious. "As if there'd be anyone for you to tell. Lucky for us, you were knocked unconscious, wiping out your shield of protection. Disposing of your unit was a simple affair after that."

"The whole...every one?" Horror registered in her expression and she shrank away from him.

A twinge of something—regret, maybe?—stirred in his gut. Why had he said that? Although eliminating the advancing enemy was their prime goal, he didn't know if Asher and the others had succeeded yet or not. He should have just kept his mouth shut.

"If...if they're all gone, why are you taking me with you? What do you want with me?" She spoke tentatively, as if she didn't really want to know the answers.

"As one with abilities, you are a very dangerous

member of your army. I cannot permit you to join up with another group to threaten the safety of my people before my men have completed their mission."

Her head snapped to attention as if she'd been struck. "Threaten? We are a danger to you?"

He wasn't impressed. "You act surprised."

Two spots of color appeared on her cheeks as she thrust a finger at him. "You're here—on our side. You're the ones who threaten us."

He closed his eyes for a moment, trying not to recall the images of his ransacked village. The charred bodies hanging from the trees. The missing children.

He shoved aside those memories and stared at this woman. She didn't look like she could be capable of such actions, and yet... "You are mistaken, little soldier."

She appeared shaken, but her tone was caustic. "You're lying, barbarian. I've seen what you've done."

He took a menacing step toward her. What arrogance that this woman called *him* the monster, as if her people were innocent of unspeakable crimes, incapable of the atrocities he'd seen with his own eyes. Maybe Asher had been right. Maybe this was a mistake.

She backed away from him, her delicate nostrils flaring. "What do you plan to do with me once we're in the Barrowlands?"

"Throw you in jail and wait for the courts to decide."

CHAPTER THREE

Remove your clothing."

"Excuse me?" She couldn't have heard him correctly with his strange accent. It sounded like—

"I said, take off your garments. All of them." The barbarian unbuckled the weapons strap that crossed diagonally over his chest and tossed it at his feet, then reached for the belt of his leather kilt.

She *had* heard him correctly. Her heart lurched as she realized he was going to force himself on her. Frantically, she looked around for a telltale mattress or a pile of blankets, but saw only hard rock and rows of small wooden boxes.

Was he going to take her like a dog? Push her up against the wall and kick her legs apart? Did he think she was going to give him oral? She ground her teeth together, hardly able to believe this was happening to her. But he was a barbarian, so why should she be surprised he was going to force himself on her? That was what they did. Rape and pillage.

Think. Think. There had to be a way out of this. Maybe she should let him *believe* she would go along with his demands, then wait for an opportunity to knee him in the balls and run like hell. But the thought of caving, even if she didn't intend to follow through willingly, was just too offensive to stomach.

"I will not."

Though he continued to unbuckle his belt, he looked up. His angular jaw was peppered with a thin layer of stubble, making it hard to tell if he normally wore a short goatee or if he'd just not shaved in a while. Even in the light, his icy blue eyes seemed fathomless, and tiny crinkles appeared at the corners.

He didn't find this amusing, did he? Determined not to appear weak, she kept her expression hard, her gaze steady—her only weapons since he'd taken her real ones away.

Then his mouth quirked.

He *did* find this funny. Her internal temperature ratcheted up and her breaths became shallow and heavy. This was her life, her wellbeing, and yet it was just a game to him. How dare he make a mockery of her situation?

"Suit yourself." He turned his back to her as if he didn't consider her a threat. At all.

We'll see about that.

She glanced around for anything she could use against him—a rock, a handful of the gritty sand underfoot, a piece of—

The muscles of his broad back flexed, catching the

light and creating shadows along his spine. Dark hair swept his shoulder blades as he fiddled with the fastenings of the few remaining garments he wore—if you could call them garments. They looked more like the medieval costumes she'd sewn for clients. The leather dropped from his hips, exposing his tight butt, and when he stepped out of the clothes on the ground, the heavily roped muscles of his thighs contracted beneath his skin.

His body was powerful and strong, his presence so commanding that she forgot who and what he was for a moment.

She needed to turn away, but it was as if she were tethered to this man by an invisible rope. Something about him felt almost familiar, as though she'd seen him before. As though they'd shared...something. Okay, that was ridiculous. She'd never even met a Cascadian, and she'd certainly never met anyone who looked like *this.*

What the hell was she thinking? Was she nuts?

Maybe that bump on the head had rattled her more than she thought. She had to put as much distance between the two of them as she could possibly manage, and then maybe, while he wasn't looking, she could take off.

Digging her fingernails into her palms, she took a step backward. Then another. And another.

"Stop. Do not move from me again." He turned to

face her with a look that said he knew exactly what she was planning.

When she glimpsed what dangled between his legs, her breath caught in her throat. Oh God, it was…wow. His flaccid length was as thick as a pipe and it hung confidently in front of his balls. Somehow, she dragged her gaze away, though it was difficult. His magnificent body was a freaking magnet to her eyeballs.

"Why... What... I will not have sex with you." She looked up in order to avoid staring at his amazing physique, but even the stalagmites or stalactites—whatever—seemed phallic. "It's not going to happen."

His laughter boomed through the tunnel, as if what she'd said was the most ridiculous thing he'd ever heard. "That is not my intention, little soldier. These garments are some of my favorites. I don't want them destroyed."

It took a moment for his words to register. Relieved that he didn't plan to force himself on her—if she could believe him—she kept her gaze averted from his brazen nudity. "I don't understand."

"What don't you understand? That I'm fond of what I'm wearing?"

"Why your clothes would be destroyed."

One of his eyebrows shot up. "Are you being serious with me?"

Why would he think she was lying?

"Don't they teach that *intelligence* over here?" He

pronounced the word as if it was foreign to him.

She had no idea what he was talking about, which made her feel a little stupid. Maybe she hadn't been paying attention during orientation like she should have. They had crammed a lot of material into the few short weeks before she was assigned to a field unit.

He rubbed a hand over his raven hair, still clearly confused. "Clothing disintegrates during the portal crossing, and I rather fancy what I had on today. But it's your choice. You can disrobe now or later. Either way, you will be unclothed when you reach the other side. Do you have any weapons on your person that I didn't find?"

"N...n...naked?" Why hadn't she heard this about the portals? It wasn't exactly a minor detail. She grabbed the lapels of her uniform, tugging them closer around her neck.

"Answer me." He acted vaguely pissed off and she didn't know why.

"Weapons? Uh, no."

Narrowing his eyes, he looked her up and down. She fidgeted under the intense scrutiny. "So you had no idea why they're called Iron Portals?"

"I...I never really thought about it."

He shook his head, as if he wasn't sure he believed her. "You are carrying no weapons other than those I found? Because if you're lying to me, soldier, you will regret it."

It occurred to her that this could be some sort of psychobabble designed to weaken her. Wasn't that the first step in breaking the enemy's will—get the prisoner to voluntarily do what you ask, like surrender any hidden weapons? "Is that a threat?"

"I don't threaten, little soldier—or play games—but if you are carrying any iron-based metals when you cross over, you could die. Believe me…death by iron sickness is not a pleasant one."

"And why should I believe that you care if I die or not?"

"I don't," he said flatly, "but as a Talent, you're valuable to us."

He propped a foot on the stone seat and folded the leather kilt he'd been wearing. Angled as he was, she caught a glimpse of what hung almost nonchalantly between his legs. Did these barbarians have no sense of modesty? Did they all parade around over there like cavemen, leaving absolutely nothing to the imagination? No wonder their worlds were so different.

She seriously needed to stop staring at him and focus on how to get out of here. And when she did, she'd alert someone to the portal location. The army had been searching for this opening for years. This could be the chance to prove to everyone that she wasn't just an annoying necessity. Surely he couldn't have killed *all* the

R-Dubs. Forty men? No way. Probably another one of his brainwashing strategies. He had to be lying in order to make her think the situation was hopeless.

He turned from her slightly, setting his things inside one of the chests. Now was her chance. Despite her bruised ribs and pounding head, she spun around and sprinted into the darkness.

"You might as well stop," he called after her. "I know you can't see well. You won't get far, and you will simply be out of breath."

Her head thunked on a stone outcropping. *Ouch.* There went her headache again.

"Or hurt yourself further. I don't want to carry you back, but believe me, I will."

What an arrogant bastard. All soldiers were—Cascadians, Pacificans—it didn't matter. It was probably a job requirement. With her hands outstretched this time, she continued forward, but it was more like a quick shuffle.

She hadn't taken more than a dozen steps when she heard his footfalls closing in behind her. Then a vise—his large hand—gripped her upper arm and yanked her around. She stumbled and crashed into him.

"Let me go." She squirmed in his arms, then pounded her fists against his bare chest, but she got nowhere. Aware that the rest of him was bare as well, she was thankful for the darkness.

Prickly heat, or maybe an icy chill—she couldn't be sure—skittered across her flesh and her heart hammered out an uneven staccato inside her ribcage. Like the pain of an injury that takes a moment to register in your brain, it took a half-second until her body and mind were filled with the strangest sensations. Her struggles became halfhearted.

A vision appeared before her like a scene from a silent film—misty and grainy—which didn't make sense. She wasn't a Psychic-Talent. She felt as if she were floating, dreaming, yet she wasn't, because her fists were jammed against the assassin's warm chest, anchoring her in this bizarre reality. She tried to push away from him, but he continued to grasp her tightly, his fingers pressing almost painfully into her triceps. A strange image came into focus in front of the stone walls.

A woman with longish blond hair and wearing a pale blue gown turned in the mist and lifted her head.

Neyla couldn't breathe. The air was a brick in her lungs.

Me? That's…me?

The woman looked exactly like Neyla. Down to the small chicken-pox scar in the middle of her forehead and the empty triple-pierced holes in her left earlobe.

Neyla's knees turned to rubber. She'd have fallen if the assassin hadn't been holding her up.

A man appeared behind the woman in the vision. A

tall man with powerful, muscular arms and raven hair that fell to his shoulders.

Oh God. Him!

The assassin exhaled slowly. Was he seeing this, too? His warm breath whispered across her cheek, fluttering a loose strand of her hair. The strength of his beating heart pounded through her fists, her arms, her body.

Neyla's breathing became ragged as she watched, unable to tear her eyes away. The man in the mist nuzzled the woman's neck, and when he ran his hands up her arms, her own flesh seemed to tingle in response. The woman's dress slipped from her shoulders, past her hips, and pooled at her feet. Neyla gasped and a tinge of embarrassment washed over her. The woman—this reflection of herself—was naked now. They both were. The man stroked the woman's breasts, her belly, her hips. Oh God, he was reaching between her legs.

Then the man in the vision lifted his head and smiled. Directly at Neyla. As if he knew she was watching.

What the hell is this? It's impossible...

The assassin's grip had loosened enough that she was finally able to push away. Instantly, the mist faded. She rubbed her arms where he'd held her a moment ago, the heat from his hands still on her skin. Neither of them said anything for several long minutes. All she heard was the frantic beating of her heart and the panting sound her breath made, as if she'd just finished a training run.

"Let's go," he said finally.

The sound of his voice knocked her out of her stupor. "Not before you tell me what you just did." Her voice cracked, making her sound desperate, but she honestly didn't care. When he didn't respond, anger rubbed along her nerve endings, the same ones that had been so titillated. "Are you going to give me an answer or not?"

"I did nothing," he replied.

"And you expect me to believe that?"

Something flashed in his eyes, only to be replaced by the hard, unbending look of a warrior glaring at his enemy. Like doors clanging shut on a train, there was no way out, no way to change things. "If you don't move now, I'm going to hoist you over my shoulder and carry you back like any respectable barbarian would do. Is that what the bloody hell you want?"

She needed no more prompting than that.

In a few minutes, they were back where they started. The man ushered her past the wooden storage boxes into a tiny stone alcove she hadn't noticed before, hardly big enough for one person. She spun around but he was right there, the heat from his naked body practically tangible. She drew the scent of him into her lungs. He smelled of soap or maybe herbal body wash, with an underlying tinge of musky maleness. If she moved a fraction, her lips would be pressed to the hollow at the base of his neck.

And he had wanted her to take off her clothes? *Yeah, right.*

Without touching her, he caged her body against the stone and the air charged with energy. A low hum, which she had mistaken for the ringing sound of silence in her ears, intensified without getting louder until it rippled like waves over her skin. The fabric of her clothing seemed to vibrate. It was only when she felt the coolness of the stone against her back and the warmth from his body on her breasts, that she realized she was completely naked.

And, of course, so was he.

* * *

The woman swayed, looking for the wall behind her for support, but it was now gone.

"Right this way." Rickert almost put his hand at the small of her back to guide her, but he stopped himself just in time. He'd seen enough arousing visions. "Welcome to the Cascadian side of the portal. Or the Barrowlands, as you seem to prefer."

He followed her closely in case she tripped, and they stepped into the antechamber.

Although she tried to cover the front of her body,

there was nothing she could do about her backside. His gaze swept over her shoulders, along the delicate channel of her spine, the soft roundness of her bottom, the dimples where he'd place his thumbs if he were to—

Heat rushed between his legs, stirring his cock. Bloody hell, what was he thinking? If she saw his erection, it would only confirm her opinion that he was just a barbarian. He didn't pause to consider why it mattered what she thought of him. It just did.

He shoved past her and was soon rummaging through the clothes in his storage trunk. Pulling out a tunic, he held it out behind him, not turning to face her.

"Here, put this on." When she didn't take it right away, he added, "Unless you'd prefer to arrive at the Crestenfahl castle completely naked."

She grabbed the tunic from him. "But aren't we in the Barrowlands? In Cascadia?"

"We are. Crestenfahl is my village."

"I...I didn't know you have castles."

"Our realm is very different from yours," he said, pulling on a pair of breeches. "In many, many ways." She'd find that out soon enough. "What's your name?"

It took her a moment to respond, as if she were trying to decide what to tell him. "Neyla Trihorn. Agent Neyla Trihorn." She held her arms around the shapeless tunic now covering her body. There was no sense of pride in her voice or her countenance, confirming his original hunch that, despite the uniform, she was no soldier. "And you are…?"

He stood and finished tying the leather laces of his fly, making sure the loops were even. When he looked up to answer, her gaze slid quickly to his face and two rosy spots colored her cheeks again. He was oddly pleased he'd caught her staring at his maleness.

"I am Rickert D'Angelus," he said proudly. "Son of Carrick D'Angelus. Leader of a band of Iron Guild warriors from Crestenfahl." He grabbed the well-worn weapons strap from the bench and cinched it diagonally across his body. Soldier or not, she was fighting for the Pacifican cause, which made her the enemy. He couldn't forget that. "And what was the purpose of your unit's mission back there in the mountains, Agent Trihorn?"

She did nothing to hide the contempt on her face. "To prevent barbarian insurgents from infiltrating further into the Pacifica realm."

"How honorable," he said sarcastically. As if her people were in that precise location only to intercept Cascadians.

"That's your point of entry into our world, isn't it?"

One of them, yes. "And your army had no other purpose for being there?"

"Isn't that enough?" She stared at him point-blank, her expressive eyes reflecting innocence, not treachery.

She spoke the truth. Or the truth as she knew it. And something inside him threatened to give way.

What the bloody hell were these soldiers being told, anyway?

Although she had an air of vulnerability, there was a mental toughness in her that he couldn't quite define. It was as if she didn't exactly belong, but wasn't about to admit it.

Rummaging through his things, he handed her a small parcel.

"What's that?" she asked, eyeing the brown paper skeptically.

"Dried *ogappa.*"

She frowned. "Never heard of it."

"It tastes somewhere between a mango and a peach. Helps calm your belly after you cross through."

Taking the package from him, she tugged at the waxy string, plucked out a small piece, and took a bite. "It's very good." She popped two more pieces into her mouth. "It's...it's helping already."

She tried to hand the package back, but he shook his head. "No, keep it. It's yours."

The small smile she gave him pulled at his insides. He could almost feel himself unraveling. It occurred to him then that she was an angelfish swimming in a sea of sharks.

Of which he was one.

"Other than your gut being unsettled, how do you feel?" He eyed the nasty bump on her forehead. It would be black and blue by morning unless it was treated. When they stopped at the Guthrie farm to pick up Duag, he'd see if one of the women could put together a healing poultice for her.

"What do you mean? I've been captured by the enemy. How *should* I feel?"

The *ogappa* must indeed be helping. The fiery nature he'd glimpsed on the other side was back. "I was referring to what that soldier did to you."

His mood darkened as he thought about the bastard. If Rickert could kill him again, but more slowly and painfully this time, he'd do it in a heartbeat. No one who hurt this woman should be allowed to die painlessly.

"Smythe thinks I'm—" The agony in her voice was a clamp around his heart, squeezing until it hurt.

He slammed shut the heavy lid of the trunk and the bang echoed loudly in the chamber. If the walls hadn't been carved out of solid rock, he'd have punched them as well. He fought the crazy urge to take her into his arms and tell her he'd protect her. Instead, he grabbed the jewel-encrusted locket—a constant reminder of what he'd lost and who was to blame—and turned it over in his hand.

This was madness. Sheer idiocy. Despite that stimulating vision, he did not care for this woman. At all. He needed to get his head out of this bloody fantasyland before it affected his judgment any further than it had already.

The powerful sensations those misty images stirred up were wrong on so many levels. They were enemies on opposite sides of an age-old war and he couldn't forget that.

"What about Smythe?" he asked.

"Never mind."

"Good. Because the bastard is dead."

CHAPTER FOUR

Dread crept up Neyla's arms as she looked around. She was really in the Barrowlands. Or as he preferred, Cascadia. Home of the enemy. Maybe she should've felt some sort of remorse that Smythe was dead, but she didn't.

The antechamber was at least twice the size of the one on the other side of the portal. Evenly spaced storage chests lined these walls, too. But they were larger, with detailed carvings on the tops and sides and ornate metal clasps and hinges. In front of each one was a small wooden bench. The center area was open—big enough for dozens of men to gather.

She shivered. This was where the insurgents staged their attacks on the Pacifica realm.

The man—Rickert—was absently fingering a jeweled pendant of some sort as he opened trunk after trunk, searching for something. Over and over he swung the cord around his finger, first one way, then the other. Light from the torches occasionally reflected off the colored stones and danced on the walls. She'd been so disoriented from the portal crossing she didn't remember that he'd lit them. At least the *ogappa* seemed to be helping. She didn't feel on the verge of puking any longer, although the butterflies remained.

As he closed yet another heavy lid, the pendant—a locket—fell from his hand and clattered to the floor. It skittered like an open clamshell across the flagstones and stopped near her feet.

"Bloody hell," he growled.

She scooped it up and handed it back to him, but not before glimpsing a miniature portrait inside of a beautiful woman with dark hair and porcelain skin.

He grabbed the piece from her and examined it closely.

"Is it broken?" she asked, trying to ignore the echo of his brief touch on the palm of her hand.

He stuffed it into his pocket. "It's fine."

"You should be less cavalier with something so fragile."

His head snapped up, fire burning behind his icy blue eyes. "What are you talking about?"

"You were swinging it around by that cord and flipping it in your hand."

"I was not."

She didn't want to argue with him. "I don't know the value of something like that over here, but it's clearly the work of a talented artisan. What is her name?"

He gave her a quizzical look.

"The woman in the locket." Clearly, she held a special

place in his heart.

"Was," he said quietly. The word hung in the air like a hangman's noose. "Maris is dead."

The simple, matter-of-fact way he said those three little words underscored the depth of his loss. "I'm...I'm truly sorry."

"I'm sure you are," he said roughly, tossing her a pair of leather boots. "Put these on."

She picked them up, but kept thinking about the woman. Was she his wife? His lover? How had she died?

"I doubt they'll fit," she said, examining the boots. They were huge.

"This isn't one of your shopping malls, Agent Trihorn. They're the smallest I could find."

He held a cotton shirt by the sleeves and wound it a few times as he approached.

She didn't like the looks of this. "What are you doing?" she asked, quickly slipping her feet into the oversized boots.

"It's a blindfold." Before she could protest, he covered her eyes with the shirt and tied the sleeves behind her head. "You don't think I'm going to let you see where you are, do you?"

Why would it matter? Unless... It occurred to her that it meant she might get out of this predicament at some point. That he was concerned she'd lead someone back here if she saw where they were going.

She held her hands out like she had in the tunnel. "But I can't even see to walk."

"I'm sure you'll manage." She jumped at the sound of his voice—he was in front of her now. Then a rope tightened around her wrists. "Better?"

"But—"

"Follow me."

The rope jerked. She had no choice but to start walking.

In a few minutes, they exited the dampness of the tunnel. Birds chirped around them, a rooster crowed somewhere in the distance, and the air smelled cool and fresh. It must be early morning here, just like it was on the other side. She found this strangely comforting. From the sound their boots made on the ground and the occasional tickle against her arms, she assumed they were trudging along a forest path. And when she felt the warmth of the sun at her back, she wondered if they were walking west.

At some point during the journey, she stumbled and caught herself by grabbing onto the back of his shirt. He let her continue on like that for a while, but when she kept stepping on his heels, he quickly tucked her fingers into the welt pocket on the back of his breeches.

"There," he said. "Hold on and stay to the side. Off my boots."

He said nothing more to her as they walked, and she

found herself silently counting the rhythmic flexing of his muscles against her fingertips.

She was actually glad her face was covered. One—he wouldn't be able to see how red her cheeks were. Physical contact may not be a big deal to him, but where she came from, people respected their personal space and certainly didn't touch strangers like *this.* And two—with her eyes covered, she wouldn't be able to see another vision, which might be triggered by touching him.

After crossing several streams and walking for what seemed like hours, they finally stopped. "Wait here." His footsteps crunched away from her on gravel.

Her heart thundered in her chest. Were they at the jail pits?

Awkwardly, with her hands bound together, she pulled off the blindfold, fully prepared to run if he had been fool enough to leave her unattended. What she saw surprised her.

A small cottage stood at the edge of the forest, a white picket fence surrounding the front yard. From this angle, she could see part of a barn and a large field behind it. Several chickens scattered out of Rickert's way as he strode down the flagstone path, and a dog barked from inside. A full-figured woman stepped out onto the porch and gave Rickert a generous hug. She wore a fuchsia, sari-like tunic that draped over one shoulder and matching pantaloons that gathered at her ankles.

It was clear they were talking, but from this distance, she couldn't quite make out what they were saying. Rickert pointed in her direction a few times. The woman glanced over, nodding her head as she listened. A moment later, she threw up her hands at something he said and stepped off the porch.

"I'll be the judge of that," the woman called over her shoulder as she came marching down the path. With her hands on her hips, and slightly out of breath, she stopped in front of Neyla.

Being an enemy combatant, Neyla wasn't sure what she should or shouldn't say to the locals, so she pressed her lips into a tight smile and examined the woman's gorgeous outfit instead. The weave of the fuchsia fabric was too fine to be cotton and yet it didn't quite look like silk, either. Complicated gold embroidery lined the neck and hemlines. The garment's seams were done with tiny, pinprick-sized stitches, making Neyla wonder if the whole thing had been hand sewn.

"You," the woman commanded in a heavy accent. "Let me see your hands."

Neyla did as she was told and held them out, noting that the woman had a presence similar to that of Captain Gravich. People like them gave orders, expecting others to comply.

The woman clucked as she untied the rope, then

turned Neyla's palms face up.

"Sorry they're so dirty," Neyla said, embarrassed. Had she realized how filthy they were, she'd have tried to wash them in the stream they crossed a few miles ago. There wasn't much she could do about it now.

"That is to be expected," the woman said gruffly. She passed a gnarled hand over Neyla's palms and briefly massaged the base of her thumbs.

Stifling a sigh, Neyla managed not to close her eyes in bliss. She loved hand massages. And foot massages, though the blisters on her heels wouldn't appreciate one right now.

"That wrist of yours came close to breaking," the woman said, letting go of Neyla's hands.

"It did?" Then she remembered falling onto the ledge. "Yes, I suppose you're right, but how did you know?" Suddenly, it dawned on her. "Are you a...healer?" The army was always looking for Healer-Talents, but she'd never met one before.

A shadow passed behind the woman's eyes. "I'm no healer, child, though I wish I were."

The sound of laughter drew Neyla's attention. She looked up to see two beautiful young women exit the cottage to join Rickert on the porch. The short, curvy one wearing a vivid blue sari handed him a large mug, and he responded by kissing her on the cheek. She must've blushed, because she held her hands to her face and laughed. The tall, willowy one wore a butter-yellow sari, but instead of pantaloons, she had on fitted, pale beige pants, possibly made of leather. She hugged him as well, and he kept a hand at her waist as he drank.

They obviously knew each other well, she thought, and for some inexplicable reason, her stomach tightened. Who were these women? Was the tall one romantically involved with Rickert? Or maybe they both were. It occurred to Neyla that she knew nothing of the customs in the Barrowlands. Did men here take several wives? Have multiple sexual partners? She turned away, not wanting to speculate further about his love life.

After examining Neyla's hands, the woman studied the rest of her as if she were trying to figure out a mathematical equation—intense thought coupled with no emotion. Neyla shifted her weight and bit her lip, unsure of what to say or do, before a peculiar sensation washed over her. A sudden prickly awareness. It was as if the woman knew her already—her history, her background—and yet, they'd barely said two words to each other. Strangely, Neyla found herself wanting to measure up to the scrutiny.

Finally, the woman broke her silence. "He knows the truth about you," she said flatly.

Okay, so Rickert had explained to her that Neyla was their enemy, but wasn't it obvious already? She rubbed a tender spot on her wrist where the rope had chafed.

"The truth?"

"Yes." The woman nodded. "He just doesn't know he knows."

* * *

"You've been smoking too much *prath,*" Rickert told Rosamund as he led Duag out of his stall. "Did Mr. Dunmire send some back with Antonia and Katla?" It certainly wouldn't surprise him. The proprietor of Crestenfahl's hookah pub was always doing little things to get Rosamund's attention. Rickert wouldn't have been surprised to learn that the man sent the young women home with some of his private stash.

She folded her arms across her chest. "I haven't touched that stuff in ages. I'm perfectly lucid."

Maybe it was a mistake to bring Neyla through the portal. He didn't need the headache.

"What are your plans for her?"

"Please, Rosa. It doesn't concern you."

He glanced at Neyla. She was sitting on the front porch of the cottage, a stone's throw away from the barn. At Rosamund's insistence, Antonia and Katla had brought food and drink for her, but they didn't stay to talk. Rubbing her wrist, Neyla bit into a crust of bread and stared out across the fields toward the forest.

A small knot formed in his gut as he thought about

how strange this must be for her, alone in a foreign land. But he knew the feeling well. Although he'd spent a fair amount of time on the other side to undermine the Pacifican army's efforts to find the Iron Portals, he'd never connected with anyone. Only the members of his small band of fighting men. But even when he came back here, he felt as if he didn't belong. Seasons changed, homes were built, crops were planted, families were started. Despite the devastating loss he'd suffered and would never forget, people around him seemed to have no problem getting right back to the business of living.

He tied Duag to a hitching ring. The stallion's black coat gleamed like polished obsidian, his long mane silky and free of tangles. Rickert really didn't need to spend much time brushing him before they headed out to Crestenfahl, but he did it anyway. The longer it took to get there, the more time he had before turning Neyla over to the jail master.

"He looks great," Rickert said, changing the subject. He didn't want to discuss Neyla's situation with Rosamund. He knew what had to be done. "Was he a good boy for you?"

The woman snorted. "A troublemaker as usual, but in the end, he did his job and did it well. Doc Murphy says all three mares are pregnant."

"Already?" Rickert laughed and patted the stallion's neck. "You were busy, weren't you, boy?"

"What did you expect?" She grabbed an old broom from the corner and knocked down a few cobwebs. "You were gone almost two months. It was plenty of time."

"Then I'd say he earned his keep."

Rosamund stopped sweeping and placed a hand on his arm. "Now. About Neyla."

Not again. He stiffened. He didn't want to be an asshole to this woman who was like a mother to him, but if she kept pushing, he might not have a choice. "You're wrong about her. She's a Protection-Talent working for the Pacifican army. If given the chance, she'd kill or betray all of us—which is why I'm taking her to the pits. Let Louis figure out what she knows."

"That bone cracker? You'd let him work his *magic* on her?"

He looked warily at the broom the older woman was holding. She looked as though she might smack him with it.

"I'm shocked you'd allow such a thing," Rosamund continued. "I thought you were a better man than that."

Her words stung like an albino scorpion, fast and painful. Honor was important to him. And he knew his responsibilities well. He was taking his prisoner to the jail pits *because* he was a good man.

Rickert shrugged off her criticism. "He's effective."

"His methods are cruel and heavy-handed. Look at her. You want to knowingly place her in Louis's care?

That girl is no enemy of Cascadia. It's as plain to me as that disrespectful scowl on your face."

Glancing over the top of Duag's back, he tried to ignore the perfect view of Neyla sitting on the porch. She wasn't alone now. At some point, Antonia had joined her, and together, they were examining what looked to be a blanket. Or maybe it was some piece of clothing.

"Why?" he asked. "Did you read her?"

He really shouldn't be surprised that Rosamund thought she could predict Neyla's future. Although, if you asked Rickert, she wasn't very effective. As much as he respected Rosa, she hadn't foretold what was going to happen to his sister's village. When it really counted, her gifts had failed.

"Not her," Rosamund answered, flicking him in the arm. "You."

* * *

Neyla watched as Rickert finished saddling his big black horse, and when he was about to put on the bridle, the older woman, who had introduced herself earlier as Rosamund, called him from the cottage.

"What now?" He made a sound of exasperation, put the stallion's halter back on, and tied him up again. "Hold this, will you?" Rickert threw her the bridle.

She grabbed it by the crown and draped the reins evenly over her arm. He narrowed his eyes, clearly recognizing that she knew how to handle the tack and had been around horses before.

"Don't get any ideas about riding away on him. Duag is a one-man horse and is highly trained. He'll either buck you off or simply turn back if I whistle. And don't pet him, either. He bites." He turned on his heel and headed to the cottage.

"You sound like a handful," Neyla said to Duag, ignoring Rickert's orders and patting the animal anyway. "The pretty ones always are." Stallions were often nippy, but she wasn't intimidated. She gave him the evil eye instead. "But if you bite me, you're toast."

Rickert and Rosamund were clearly arguing about something, but Neyla could only hear snippets of the conversation.

—filthy—

—pig-headed—

—dangerous—

Rosamund held up a small package and patted her forehead. Rickert tried to snatch it from her but she jerked it away.

—crazy—

—jail pit—

Absolutely not.

In the end, he crossed his arms over his chest,

looking bored as Rosamund talked animatedly to him.

A few minutes later, with the package tucked into his belt, he strode back into the barn. Without saying a word, he put the bridle on Duag—a little roughly, if you asked her—and offered Neyla a leg up. She brushed his hand away, checked the girth, and cinched it a little tighter, scolding Duag when he stomped a hoof.

"Front or back?" she asked.

Rickert stood there, hesitating. "What?"

"Will you be riding in front of me or behind me?"

"You...you know horses." It wasn't a question, really, since he'd recognized earlier that she was familiar with them. But the fact still seemed to puzzle him. Maybe he was surprised at her confidence.

"A few, yes. Front or back?" she repeated, trying not to let her smugness show. She liked being under estimated.

"Uh, front."

"Okay then. Up you go. I'll climb on behind you."

As they rode along in silence, Neyla was grateful she'd ridden a lot as a girl. Using only her legs, she could easily maintain her seat and balance behind him without having to hold on to his waist—because, if she were honest with herself, the less physical contact she had with him, the better.

Rickert seemed strangely subdued. At least on the way to Rosamund's, he'd told her to watch her step and guided her around various obstacles in her way. Now that they were riding, he was all but silent.

"Duag is a beautiful animal," she said to break the quiet. "You keep him with Rosamund when you're...on our side?"

"Yes, and I keep her and her daughters supplied with Vengold silk from my travels."

Ah, so the fabric was a type of silk. "Do all the women here dress like that?"

He shrugged. "Some do. Others wear dresses. Fewer wear pants."

"Why? Is it forbidden?" In a male-dominated society, it shouldn't surprise her that women were forced to wear dresses or saris to cover their legs. If a woman exposed them, they probably assumed she was a whore.

He glanced over his shoulder at her and frowned. "We have no rules like that. I think they prefer to dress that way."

"So if I walked through your streets wearing shorts and a tank top, I wouldn't be jailed... or pulled into a dark corner and raped?"

Reining Duag to a halt, he turned in the saddle to stare at her. Up this close, she couldn't help breathing in the herbal soap smell of his sun-warmed skin. "We have our customs, Agent Trihorn, just like you do over there, but violence against women is never acceptable. However, I suspect the punishment we mete out for such crimes is much more final."

He wasn't quite angry with her, she decided. It was more like...disappointment or hurt. She suddenly felt myopic and foolish, aware that she was judging his world—perhaps too harshly—through her own limited lens.

"I'm...sorry. That was unfair of me."

A tiny muscle in his jaw flexed. "Clearly, you've got a biased view of me and my people."

As she stared down at her hands, she knew he was right. She'd never bothered to learn anything about them other than what she'd gathered from scattered news reports and army briefings. Occasionally, the tabloids would have a story about someone crossing over, but there were some in her world who didn't even believe the portals existed. She recalled a well-known evangelist who publicly stated he wanted to save the barbarians, so he prayed for a portal to be shown to him. As far as she knew, it had never happened, because he was soon preaching about how the portals and the Barrowlands weren't real. They were merely the unholy inventions of a society in moral decline that was fixated on false prophets and the supernatural.

"Yes, I guess that's true," she admitted.

He was quiet for a moment, contemplating what she'd just said. "But I'm sure I'm just as guilty of judging you." The way he said it made it sound so personal, as if the rift between their worlds boiled down to just the two of them.

It was easier to be angry with him for being part of the enemy as a whole. It was less easy to be upset with him, the man. After all, he had saved her from Smythe and had shown remarkable concern for her welfare. He'd even given her the package from Rosamund, explaining that it was a poultice of herbs to help with the bruising.

The saddle leather squeaked as he shifted slightly, and she assumed he was about to turn around. Instead, he reached back and carefully moved a strand of hair from her face without touching her skin. Only when his gaze dropped to her mouth did she realize she'd licked her lips, drawing his attention.

"My little soldier, what am I to do with you?"

The air around them seemed to crackle. She was suddenly hot under the thin tunic. Could she be reading him right? Was he going to kiss her? Should she lean forward a couple of inches and kiss him first? She wondered what he'd taste like, how his skin would smell if she were that close. Would his short stubble prickle against her lips?

Duag stomped an impatient foot and snorted, effectively breaking the spell.

The corner of Rickert's mouth twisted. "I suppose if it were *me* walking down *your* streets wearing my leather kilt, I'd draw a few stares too."

She laughed at the visual, relieved on some level that whatever had just happened between them was over.

"Yeah, from every woman with a set of eyeballs." She remembered his bare, muscular chest. His powerful shoulders and arms. Women would line the streets in New Seattle just to admire his physique. After all, who could resist a man like him, wearing nothing but a leather kilt?

CHAPTER FIVE

"We're not far now," Rickert said, startling Neyla.

She must have dozed off for a bit, lulled to sleep by the rhythmic sound of Duag's hoofs on the hard-packed ground. Stifling a yawn, she had no idea how he knew where they were, since she couldn't see for more than a few feet given the thick fog. Shadows just out of reach hovered in the mist, mere hints of the trees and bushes around them. Once, she thought she saw something moving, but when she blinked a few times and stared harder, it was gone.

She leaned a little closer to Rickert's broad back.

"You okay, lass?" he said over his shoulder.

His concern touched her more than she was willing to admit. "I'm...I'm fine. Just tired and loopy, I guess."

"That is to be expected. Your first crossing through an Iron Portal can be exhausting and overwhelming."

"How many times have you crossed over?" she asked, trying to be more conversational than probing.

"Often enough." His clipped answer didn't surprise her. Telling her specifics like that would be sharing secrets with the enemy.

As she listened to the steady clip-clop of the horse's hooves, she considered her own secrets—the lingering trauma of the train wreck that was never far from her thoughts. The guilt. The horror. Some things were best left alone, where they would hopefully be forgotten.

At least in theory, that's how things were supposed to work.

A short time later, Rickert reined Duag to a stop at the edge of the forest. The fog had thinned somewhat. "There it is. Crestenfahl Castle."

Following the direction he was pointing, she saw a stone fortress rising out of the mist. It appeared to be floating above the clouds.

She must've gasped because he added, "It's beautiful, isn't it?"

"Y…yes," she managed to say. "I've never seen anything like it."

Then, before she could balance herself or grab the saddle, he urged Duag into a canter. She nearly lost her seat, and she had no choice but to wrap her arms around his waist. He'd done this several times throughout the journey. She was beginning to think he was doing it on purpose.

The castle loomed larger as they approached and she could see that it actually sat atop a small hill overlooking a valley. Ornate corbels supported the rounded turrets of the keep and a pair of stone griffins flanked the gatehouse entryway. A tower with narrow arched windows stood at each corner of the thirty-foot wall that surrounded the courtyard.

As they rode up the narrow road, both sides of the heavy gate swung open slowly.

"Say nothing," Rickert told her. "Not even if you are asked a question. I'll handle everything."

Three dark-haired livery boys ran up to greet them. Rickert swung a leg over and hopped down. Before Neyla could do the same, he reached up, gripped her by the waist, and helped her dismount.

Although it probably seemed like a natural gesture to him, it felt intimate and thoughtful to her. Like a man opening her car door. Certainly she was capable of doing it herself, but it was nice to know he was thinking about her first.

"Can we take him for you, sir?" the tallest boy asked.

Rickert tossed him the reins. "He is to be rubbed down by hand. The tack cleaned and oiled. Think you can handle it?"

"Yes, sir," the two older children chimed together and Rickert handed them each a coin. "Remember, though—he'll bite if you're not careful."

The younger one, who couldn't be more than six or seven, dropped his chin, clearly disappointed he had not been given a job, too.

But before he could follow the other two, Rickert

pulled him aside and knelt on one knee. "We've been riding all day and Duag's going to need an extra pitch-fork of hay. Can you make sure he gets it?"

The boy straightened, his eyes brightening. "Yes, sir."

"Mr. Riley can be crabby about such things," Rickert said with an exaggerated frown. "It might be a difficult task."

"Don't worry. He's sleeping. I can do it right now before he wakes up."

Oh God, he had the most adorable lisp. She wanted to squeeze him and tell him how cute he was.

"I knew I could count on you." Rickert handed him a coin and the child ran off to join the others.

"You're very astute," she said as they crossed the courtyard and approached the keep. He knew just what to say to make each boy feel special and needed.

Rickert merely grunted and walked faster. She practically had to run to keep up.

They stopped in front of a large wooden door. The hinges groaned loudly as he pulled it open, and they stepped into a great hall. At least three stories tall, the room had a wood-beamed ceiling and colorful tapestries on the walls depicting castles, hunting scenes, and battles. Five or six candlelit chandeliers hung above one long table, where at least a dozen people stared at them. The stringed notes from a fiddle or small guitar died in the air as the door closed behind them.

"Rickert, my man, what a surprise." A tall, rosy-cheeked man dressed in leather breeches and a deep navy tunic pushed away from the table and approached. "We didn't expect you back so soon. And who have you brought home with you this time?"

This time?

Rickert pointed to a nearby bench. "Wait here."

As he strode to meet the man, several children ran up to him and gathered around his legs. He scooped up the smallest, a boy no older than four or five, and twirled him around.

Rickert and the man spoke for a few minutes, while the gaze of every other pair of eyes settled on her. Drawn to the vivid colors of the women's gowns—sapphire, aubergine, garnet, maize—she flashed a weak smile, the kind you use when being cordial to a stranger on the street. None of the women smiled back.

So much for pleasantries. Clutching her own garment tightly about her, she examined the wood bench instead and awaited her fate.

"Lord Tierney D'Angelus," Rickert said, addressing the man, "I'd like to present Miss Neyla Trihorn. Neyla, this is my uncle. The Lord of Crestenfahl."

Miss? Not Agent? Jumping to her feet, Neyla opened her mouth to say something, but Rickert gave a quick shake of his head. Lord D'Angelus bowed in her direction, but that was all. She was perplexed at the strange introduction.

Not quite what she expected for someone heading to the...jail pits.

* * *

On a set of stone steps that curved up and away from the main hall, Neyla thought she might explode. "You told him *what*?"

"Keep your voice down." Rickert kept climbing.

"But—"

"Unless you prefer to sleep on the floor of a rat-infested jail pit with nothing but a single piece of cloth to keep you warm..." His voice trailed off, as if he were defying her to argue. "I made the assumption you'd rather stay here. That you'd prefer my company to that of vermin. Was I mistaken?"

Her throat tightened further. "But...you told him we were *betrothed*?"

"Yes," he said simply, like it was no big deal.

Was this how things worked here? Was she a spoil of war now, to be used in any way he chose? Then she remembered what Lord D'Angelus had said. Rickert clearly *had* done this sort of thing before.

She glanced around the narrow passage for a way to escape, but there was nowhere to go except up or down. Not much of a choice.

If she could get away, where would she go? All she knew was that the portal was located somewhere east of here. Maybe she could steal a horse and head to Rosamund's. Even though it was a long ride, she might be able to find her way there. But then what? Would the woman take her to the portal? Although Neyla's intuition told her that Rosamund actually liked her and had been her advocate with Rickert, she doubted the woman would help her to that extent. A warm meal, maybe.

"If I'd told him the truth about who you are, he'd have sent you to the pits. And because I wouldn't bring a woman to this side simply for a wee bit of fun between the quilts, they must believe we are to marry."

She frowned. "Why do you care where I sleep or end up?"

He stopped several steps above her and turned around. For a split second, she found herself looking straight at those perfectly tied laces, before she wrenched her gaze up to his.

"Most folk are very distrustful of Pacificans. I'm trying to make it more believable that you're here."

He still hadn't answered her question. Cranking her neck back, she did her best to glare at him, but his height was even more intimidating. Without thinking, she climbed a few steps and brushed past him, then turned to look down at him. She liked this vantage point much better. It still didn't add up that he—

A corner of his mouth twitched. Something not quite frightening, but very exciting, flashed in those arctic blue eyes of his.

A warning? A promise?

Unwanted shivers cascaded down her arms, warming her insides. What was it about this man that so enticed her? He was the last man on earth she should be attracted to. Yet looking at him now, with his square jaw, broad shoulders, and strong, muscular arms, how could she not? He was beyond hot.

The crimson tunic he'd thrown on at the portal was simple and functional, yet elegant at the same time. Although it had none of the fancy embroidery or adornments that Lord Tierney's or Rosamund's garments sported, it fit his muscular torso perfectly, as if it had been hand-tailored. The hemline hit just below his natural waistline, right at the crisscrossed laces of the fine leather breeches—probably deerskin, if she were to guess—that stretched tightly over his—

She coughed and attempted to put her mind into its former work mode: fabric, cut, and fit. When she'd tailored men's clothing, she'd often kneel and hold her tape measure right at the crotch. She was used to examining and assessing various bodies simply as shapes, marking how much of the seam to take in or let out. Where to position a dart or tuck.

The leather clung to the curve of his thighs and butt

with just the right amount of ease—neither too tight nor too loose. Whoever had made them was very skilled. Leather, particularly deerskin, could be tricky to work with.

Enough about the clothes, she told herself. God, she could get so distracted by pretty things.

She was sure of one thing, though. If she had any hope of getting back home, she needed to squelch her physical reaction to him and keep her wits about her.

Then she realized he now blocked her only escape, and she had nowhere to go but up. No wonder he was pleased. She'd made it easy for him. God, she could be such an idiot.

"And why should you care what happens to me?" she repeated.

He propped one boot casually on the step above him and rested a hand on the hilt of one of his swords, looking very much like the powerful medieval warrior he was. "I agree. It makes no sense."

"Then why?"

He shrugged. "Perhaps I've been bespelled."

She scoffed at him and yet her whole body went numb at the thought that *he* could be bespelled by *her*.

Before she could contemplate further, he said, "Keep going. It's not far now."

Soon, they stood in front of a wooden door with a large metal ring for a handle. After sliding back the bolt,

Rickert leaned into it with his shoulder and pushed. The hinges creaked as the heavy door slowly opened. She wouldn't be able to manage it easily on her own.

The first thing she spotted in the elaborately furnished room was the huge, curtained bed, piled high with quilts and pillows. An empty tub, half hidden by a curtain, stood in a far corner, and several large parchments—maps, maybe?—were scattered on a low table. The room was decidedly masculine. His bedchamber.

And now it all made perfect sense.

"Is this elaborate scheme of yours designed to get me into your bed?" She glanced around for some sort of weapon and spotted several glass paperweights in various colors holding the maps flat. Those could work. In college, she'd pitched on an intramural co-ed softball team and could throw a decent fastball.

"What are you talking about?" he asked.

She inched closer to the table. "Do you have an old-fashioned belief system over here that prevents you from shagging a woman you're not engaged to?"

He closed the door with a bang that rattled her insides, and slid the bolt into place. Standing there like he had in the cave, taking up all the available space, he looked big and formidable. She was trapped. This was it. And she'd just provoked him. *Stupid, stupid, stupid.*

"Stay away from me." She lunged toward the table and grabbed what she thought was a paperweight, though it turned out to be a bulbous candleholder with a lump of wax inside. The map curled without its weight at the corner, but not before she caught a glimpse of the familiar Pacifica coastline. This must be where he planned his raiding strategies.

"You can put that down. I'm not going to hurt you."

She eyed him critically. The periwinkle-blue glass she held was fairly heavy and would inflict damage if she hit her target.

"Besides, little soldier," he continued, "I would not be happy if it broke. Those are the only pieces of Esmeralda glass I have left, and I had to trade a decent Balkirk steel blade to get them."

"Then why all the tricks?"

"Tricks?"

"Those sex visions. Did you think they'd get me hot for you and I'd agree to this betrothal nonsense?"

He blew out a long, slow breath and leaned against the door frame. "Ah, then it's true."

She was confused. "What's true?"

"In that vision. You saw us making love, too. I'd wondered what it was you'd seen, but it's clear we both witnessed the same thing."

"Yeah, how could I miss it? You were—I was—" She was so frustrated, she could hardly think straight, but she wasn't about to verbalize what she'd seen.

He frowned, scrubbing a hand thoughtfully over his

jaw. He seemed just as perplexed and confused as she was. That is, if she was reading him correctly.

And then it dawned on her. "You mean…you…you didn't do that on purpose?"

Anger flashed behind his eyes. "Me? You think I caused that to happen? That I conjured it up or something?"

"I…uh…assumed it was you." But if he didn't create those visions, what were they? She recalled the way he'd held her so tightly in the tunnel, his labored breathing, his pounding heart. It occurred to her that he'd just said *making love,* not *screwing* or *fucking.*

"Believe me," he said, "even if I had such talents, I wouldn't need to resort to trickery like that to bed women."

His flippant, confident tone struck a chord and, for a moment, she forgot about the mist. "I still won't agree to this arrangement."

Striding past her with the ease of a man used to getting his way, he flung open the heavy draperies and bright sunlight illuminated the room. He made a show of fluffing a few of the colorful pillows propped on that monstrosity of a bed, causing dust motes to dance in the light.

"You'd pick sleeping on a cold stone floor to this?" he asked, the criss-crossed swords on his back clanking as he spread his arms wide. "It's the finest Vengold silk.

And the bed is stuffed with river goose down. The best."

It did look soft, and she was very— No. She would not let herself be charmed like this. "I will not let you suck me into a game with you."

Neyla stood there with as much dignity as she could muster. If a suit could make a man, being naked under an oversized tunic and wearing big clunky boots definitely did not make a woman. At least, not a confident one. Maybe if she were wearing army fatigues or even jeans and a T-shirt, she wouldn't be feeling so unsettled. But all she had of herself on this side of the portal was her wits. And right now, they felt pretty thin.

"This is no game," he countered. "Stop being so stubborn. In the brig, you'd get maybe one pan of water—cold water—every few days in which to wash up. Despite your current appearance, you do seem to value good hygiene."

She stifled a laugh. *Yeah, I suppose that's true.*

His gaze roamed up and down her body. She willed herself to stand taller.

"And depending on whether or not there are other prisoners in the pits, the wash water may be shared among several of you."

She swallowed nervously. Other prisoners? To hell with sharing bath water. Would they be sharing her? Her resolve was quickly fading.

"You'd honestly prefer *that* to *this*?" he asked

mockingly. "I can have the house maids bring in warm water and scented oils for a bath." He removed the cork from one of the tiny bottles on his dressing table and held it to his nose. "Heatherwood is my personal favorite, but there are others you may enjoy more. I can ask Tierney's daughters for their suggestions."

God, how her muscles ached. A warm bath would be heavenly. She'd sink up to her neck in lightly scented water, close her eyes and wash away the—

Wait. He wanted her to use his favorite scent? She was suddenly reminded of a former customer who'd tried on a medieval costume she'd made for him. He'd burst from the dressing room and exclaimed, "Bathe her and bring her to me." His girlfriend and the other couple with them had erupted in laughter. It was funny at the time, but there was nothing funny about Rickert's implication of the very same thing.

"I will not share a bed with you. Or service you."

"Service?"

"You know? Sex. Like your stallion servicing the mares at the Guthrie farm in exchange for room and board."

One corner of his mouth twitched and a devilish gleam sparkled in his eyes. "I do not need to make such elaborate arrangements to bed women. They come willingly or not at all."

She reluctantly admitted to herself that he was

probably telling the truth. He was the most attractive man she'd ever seen and certainly she wasn't the only female who thought this way. Given the images in the mist and what she'd glimpsed of him at the portal crossing, it was obvious the pleasures his body would bring to a woman. Sex for him wasn't a question. The question was, with whom would he choose to have it? A man like him would have plenty of options.

"This betrothal business is the only way to keep you from the pits. If the people here knew the truth about you, that's where you'd go. While it is acceptable for a man to lie with his future bride—in fact, some here would say consummation after a betrothal constitutes marriage—it is not a requirement. I'll have the adjoining bedchamber prepared for me. You will stay here in this room, as it is better appointed."

She glanced around the room again. If he wasn't here with her, maybe she could figure out a way to escape. There was the one door they'd come in and another on the far wall, which probably led to the adjoining room. The window was plenty big enough to climb through, but she had no idea how high off the ground they were. Or where the room was in relation to those thirty-foot walls.

"And just so you know...in addition to having excellent night vision, we barbarians have excellent hearing as well. If you try to run again, I'll know it, and I'll take you to the pits myself."

"What are you talking about?" she asked, feigning innocence.

His laughter filled the whole room. "Save your breath. You're a terrible actress."

"And if I don't agree?

"Same thing. You'll go to the pits and await trial."

She tried to keep her hands from shaking, but failed miserably. She didn't want to ask, but had to. "And what kind of punishments are handed out in situations like this?"

"Generally, imprisonment, torture...death."

The muscles in her legs seemed to fail her all at once and she felt herself slipping. The fear she'd felt when she first encountered him in the cave engulfed her again. Before she could steady herself on the edge of the dresser, strong hands gripped her arms, easing her down on a nearby chair.

Instantly, another one of those misty visions began to take shape.

Rickert cursed and quickly released his hold.

The mist disappeared, but not before she'd seen a glimpse of two pairs of intertwined bare legs.

Moving away from her, he flexed his fists as if he wanted to punch something. It looked as though he was warring with himself...and losing. "This is fucked."

"Tell me about it." She wasn't sure whether he was

referring to the visions or— "Why the lies, Rickert? Why not just send me to the pits?"

He took several long breaths. She could almost hear him thinking. When he finally broke the silence, his voice was so quiet she had to strain to hear him. "Because you don't belong there."

"I...don't?"

"The magistrate owes me a favor. When the court comes to town next month, I will tell her the truth and petition her to let you return home. But the only way she'll agree is if you promise never to join your army again."

Disappointment weighed heavily on her shoulders. She wouldn't have a choice. Once she returned to New Seattle, the army would put her back in the field. "I...I'm afraid I can't make that promise. Even if I wanted to leave the army—which I do—they would force me to stay."

For some reason, it hadn't occurred to her to lie and agree to his conditions. She just wanted to get out of this whole mess. Away from here. Away from the army. And yet...

"Why do you care about me, anyway?" she asked, suddenly curious. "Because, technically, I'm your enemy."

"Bloody hell, lass! Why must you be so difficult?" For a moment, she thought he might throw something. "I don't want you to go to the pits. Does it have to be any more complicated than that?"

"But I'm—"

"Stop." He held up his hands, his eyes blazing. "It doesn't make sense, but you are not to question me further."

His patronizing tone made her insides pucker, like swallowing a shot of vinegar. "Fine. If you promise not to touch me again—I don't want to see another one of those damn visions—then I'll agree to these sleeping arrangements."

His boots pounded the floor as he approached. The small bottles on his dressing table rattled. Assuming he was going to grab her, she gripped the candleholder tighter. But he strode across the room without making contact, stirring up a breeze as he passed. He yanked the door open and turned around. His expression reminded her of the first time she'd seen him on the other side of the portal. Dangerous, frightening and foreign.

CHAPTER SIX

Using the excuse that Neyla was exhausted from the portal crossing and needed her rest, it was several days before the two of them shared a meal with the others in the Great Hall.

In truth, Rickert hadn't wanted to deal with her questions because he had no answers. He felt protective of her, though it made no sense. He wanted to be with her, even though a Warrior of the Iron Guild shouldn't want such a thing. Besides, the thought of her in the pits with Louis made him physically sick. The bone cracker would interrogate her about her army's movements and plans, using the cruelest of methods. After being chastised by Rosamund for even considering sending Neyla there, he accepted that she was right, even though he hated to admit it.

"Rickert, how is my brother doing? Staying out of trouble, I hope."

He turned to see his cousin's wife, Petra, approaching. "Hello, gorgeous," he said, giving her a kiss on both cheeks. "Fallon arrived safely and his first mission went well. Asher is keeping him in line." His gaze dropped to her pregnant belly. "Praise the Fates, you've changed since I saw you last."

"Edon's potent seed will do that to a girl," she said, laughing. She turned to Neyla. "And you must be the woman everyone is talking about. I'm Petra. I'm married to one of Lord Tierney's sons. Rickert is my cousin-in-law. Welcome to Crestenfahl." Her tone was warm and genuine.

Neyla glanced quickly at Rickert, then smiled and shook the young woman's outstretched hand. "Thank you so much."

"That dress is lovely on you," Petra said, scrutinizing the low-cut garment. "I didn't fill out a bodice like that until I was pregnant. You know, these—" She lifted one of her own breasts. "—get larger when you're pregnant before anything else does. I must say, Edon is really enjoying them. And I am, too."

A laugh burst from Neyla's mouth. Although she was clearly shocked at the woman's candor, Rickert sensed that she wasn't put off by it. "So I've heard. I designed a wedding gown for a woman who told me the same thing. When is the baby due?"

"If my calculations are correct, in a fortnight or two."

The two women launched into an easy conversation about family, clothes, and life on both sides of the portal as if they were long-lost friends.

He'd told everyone that he and Neyla were in love, having met while he'd been on a lengthy assignment in

Pacifica. Explaining that she was from one of the southern regions with fewer tensions between the worlds, he'd hoped there'd be less distrust of her. Petra notwithstanding, given the angry scowls and furtive glances they'd received from a few of the others as they entered the Great Hall, it was clear he hadn't completely succeeded.

After taking their seats at the table, Rickert was about to dish up Neyla's plate when she reached for the ladle first.

"Everything looks delicious," she said, checking out the stew.

His mouth dropped open as she scrutinized each platter of food that passed in front of them, picking out the best pieces, and placed them on his plate first.

What the hell was she doing? He hadn't told her that among his people, serving food to each other was a sign of deep affection. Given the hushed whispers among a few of the women, including Petra, they'd noticed, too.

Bollocks. He recalled the *ogappa* he'd given her at the portal without even thinking about it—as if it was the most natural thing for him to do.

"'Tis quite a shiner you gave your woman, Rickert," Big Thom said, breaking the unusual silence. Meals were normally much livelier, with the minstrel playing, and people laughing and singing. "She get out of line and you had to set her right?"

Rickert's hand stopped, suspended halfway between the plate and his mouth. His skin pricked with anger as he glared across the table. Using dirty fingers, Big Thom wiped a trickle of broth from his chin and eyeballed Neyla.

She gingerly touched the left side of her face, still bruised from her fall from the cliff.

"Guess I'd lose my temper around a seasider too, no matter how bonnie she was between the quilts."

Rickert dropped the spoon with a clank and kicked over his chair as he jumped to his feet. Neyla's concerned expression made him actually consider sitting back down.

"Look at that," Big Thom said, laughing. "Is it possible she's tamed the mighty Rickert? Or maybe it's just some trick to infiltrate the enemy. What lies beneath those skirts, lass? Must be mighty sweet indeed."

"You sonofabitch." Rickert leaped onto the table, causing platters of food to lurch. He tromped over to Big Thom and grabbed the surprised man by the collar. The first blow broke Big Thom's nose. The second knocked him backward off his chair. "You will not speak to her like that again. If you do, I'll not be so gentle with you the next time."

Though Neyla kept her gaze fixed on her plate, a hint of a smile graced her lips. And when Rickert hopped off the table and returned to his seat, her cheeks were flushed a lovely shade of pink. He'd expected her to cower away from him, but she actually inched closer. Had she liked what he had done? It wasn't the first time he'd broken Big Thom's nose and it probably wouldn't be the last. This wasn't too barbaric and uncivilized for her?

Conversation at the table was a little less subdued after everything was put back together, but it still wasn't quite normal. Big Thom wasn't the only one who didn't trust Neyla. Despite Petra's warm welcome, many of the Crestenfahl residents were on edge. Glancing around the table, Rickert noticed his cousin, Edon, caressing his pregnant wife's breasts. He couldn't see Petra's hand, but he imagined it was resting on the man's laces.

Of course. What a brilliant idea.

They needed to see Rickert treat Neyla as any man would his future bride, and until he did so, they wouldn't fully trust her.

He waited until Neyla set down her tankard of ale, then he grabbed her waist and swept her onto his lap. She gasped, opening her mouth to protest, but he silenced her with his lips.

Ah, yes, they were softer and more pliable than he'd imagined. And she smelled of heatherwood oil.

He grabbed a fistful of her hair and—what the hell, might as well make it a good show—cupped her breast through the low-cut bodice. His cock swelled as she let out a squeal of protest and squirmed against him. He heard a few chuckles.

God, he loved an audience.

"Better act like you like it, lass," he whispered, "or they'll never believe you."

"What the hell do you think you're doing?" Her voice hissed in his ear.

If they were naked right now, with her straddled over his lap like this, he'd be buried deep inside her, teasing her nipple with his tongue. But since he'd promised her he wouldn't come to her bed, this was as close as he was going to get.

"Aye, we are a bit barbaric around here."

"For God's sake, what kind of people are you?"

"We're a passionate people, Neyla, unafraid to express ourselves openly. Haven't you figured that out yet? Now act like you want me and make it believable."

One minute she was struggling against him and the next she was molding her body to his, sliding her arms around his neck. *Now that's more like it.* He stroked her thigh through the thick layers of her skirts and scooted her bottom closer.

People finally started talking—even the minstrel began to play.

Bloody hell, if only—

Neyla sucked his earlobe into her mouth, sliding her

teeth over it, and he groaned. His erection strained further against his leather breeches, pressing into the softness between her legs. It was torturous that he was this close to her but not inside. He groped for the hem of her skirts. Someone whooped, egging him on.

Then she bit down, hard.

He yelped.

"Shhh," she whispered against his throbbing earlobe. "Don't you want to make it believable?"

* * *

"Are all female Talents as sinister as you are, lass?" Rickert rubbed his ear as they entered the bedchamber several hours later.

Good, she was glad he still hurt. Served him right for pawing her like that in front of everyone. Next time, it wouldn't be just his earlobe. "Only when provoked, but then I don't know many other Talents, so I couldn't tell you."

"Aye, provoked. Just as I was." He plopped onto the bed as if he planned to stay awhile.

"Excuse me? You were provoked? The only thing you were provoked by was your over-aggressive tendencies, that pea-brain between your legs, and your exhibitionist nature." She didn't want to think about how his defense of her at dinner made him even more enticing. And for God's sake, if she had any sort of sense, she shouldn't be thinking about—

He laughed and her face grew hotter. Flexing her fists open and closed, she wanted to throw something. Where were those candleholders, anyway?

"Ah, now that's the reaction I've been itching for. That subservient behavior—although I appreciated your obedience at dinner—just doesn't suit you."

Obedience? The word stuck in her craw like a barbed thorn and she pointed toward the door. "Out. Am-scray. Get into your own room."

Ignoring her, Rickert tried to pull off his boots, but his foot kept slipping from his knee. How many tankards of ale had he had?

Oh, for heaven's sake. She grabbed the heel of one of his boots, yanked hard, then pulled off the other one. Marching across the floor, she threw them into the other room.

"You must admit, it worked," he mused. "People began to relax after that."

"Well, I'm so glad you chose to inform me of that important tidbit ahead of time. Do all men here act like testosterone-loaded teenagers?"

Without answering, he rose from the bed looking steadier than she expected, and opened the window. Cool night air filtered into the room. He stared into the darkness for a few moments, his hands braced on either side of the window frame, before he turned back to face her. "What do you mean, you've never met many other Talents before?"

She sat at the dressing table and fiddled with one of the small bottles lined up along the back. "My Talent was latent until last year, so it's only been recently that I knew I had abilities." She didn't look up when he brushed past her.

"A year? You've been a soldier for only a year?" The sound his feet made on the creaky wood floor was surprisingly intimate.

"Yeah. Surprised?"

"Actually, no." He poured himself a cup of water from a serving pitcher near the door. "It makes perfect sense. I should've guessed as much. You're no soldier."

She jerked her head up. That was something Smythe would've said. "What the hell do you mean by that?"

"Bollocks. That sounded insulting, didn't it? I'm sorry." He rubbed his forehead and flashed her a rueful smile. "What I meant to say was that your eyes don't have the dead look of a war-weary soldier. You have the eyes of a creator, someone who sees the beauty in things, not a destroyer."

"I...I do?" she said, stunned at his assessment.

"I'd have to imagine that witnessing death and destruction is particularly difficult for you."

She sat back and blinked a few times as his words

echoed in her head. It wasn't as if she didn't know this about herself. He was right. Death and destruction did bother her. Deeply.

Like clockwork, the horror of the train wreck came crashing into her thoughts.

A young boy's crumpled body, his mother sobbing next to him. Blood splattered on a subway kiosk. A man missing an arm. The sirens. The smoke.

She shoved those too-vivid memories aside.

What surprised her was that this man, whom she'd met not long ago, had summed her up so accurately.

Rising from her seat, she strolled to the window and gazed into the darkness. Without electric lights from any city, the constellations were brighter here, more significant. She easily found Cassiopeia and Orion.

She smiled inwardly, relieved that she wouldn't have to lump him into the same asshole category as Smythe. For some reason, she didn't want there to be any similarities between the two men, even though they were both soldiers. Rickert could make her infuriatingly angry, and yet he could be incredibly astute.

"What did you do before the army?" he asked from behind.

"Nothing. It's not important."

"I want to know." His tone was soft, but insistent.

"But—"

"Tell me."

Very well. What was the harm? "I started a clothing design business after college. It's gone now. They wouldn't—I couldn't do both."

"They made you give it up," he said quietly, guessing the truth. "Was that difficult?"

She shrugged. "It was a silly endeavor anyway."

"Bloody hell, lass."

She glanced over her shoulder. He looked genuinely pissed off.

"You owned your own business," he continued. "You created something beautiful that people desired, using only your hands and your imagination."

A little piece of her insides melted. She suddenly wanted to tell him more of what she used to do. "We did a lot of theater work and parties. A few weddings. Some of the stuff we did was so..." She turned back to the window. *Worthless,* her father would've said.

"Theater work, Neyla? How interesting."

She liked how he said her name, as if he'd been saying it for years.

"There's a festival every summer where all the local artisans gather and—" His voice fell. "Well, of course, you'll be gone by then."

They were both quiet for a moment and she attempted to swallow past the lump in her throat. She should be happy that she'd be home, but somehow she wasn't.

"Do you miss it?" he asked finally. "Your shop?"

She nodded, but didn't trust herself to speak. There was no point in telling him that seeing the beautiful garments and fabrics over here reminded her just how much she missed that part of her life.

He came up behind her, his presence heating her skin. "May I? You will never get these wee buttons unfastened." Without waiting for a reply, his fingers brushed her neck as he swept her hair to the front. "I remember when I bought this, on one of my journeys to the South."

"You...you bought this?" For whom? she wanted to ask, but couldn't. When he'd brought the gown to her earlier, she'd assumed he'd borrowed it from someone. Her stomach twisted knowing she was wearing something he'd originally purchased for one of his lovers. Had he undressed someone else like this? Was that why he knew these buttons were difficult?

"Not the gown, the fabric," he corrected. "Along with many of the other things we can't get here. When I'm not...on duty, I travel a lot and pick up things the people of Crestenfahl need. Lord Tierney's wife and daughters make clothing to sell at the various markets and festivals, and I bought this bolt of fabric for them."

Relieved that she wasn't wearing a former lover's cast-offs, she closed her eyes and concentrated on the feel of his fingers as they moved along her spine. His breath whispered against her skin and goosebumps prickled her arms. She hadn't expected a warrior to have such a gentle touch. The time and care he took with each button felt deliberate. As though he was waiting for her to explode with desire.

Well, it was working.

When he spoke again, his voice was a hoarse whisper. "I had no idea I'd see it...like this. I picked the dress out in the market yesterday, hoping it'd fit."

She was strangely touched that he'd bought this specifically for her.

By the time he got to the final button, a trail of need stretched from the nape of her neck and down the curve of her back. Would he slide the dress from her shoulders now? Would she cave and make love to him if he did?

A delicious heat pooled low in her belly. Of course she would. Why try to deny it? He hooked his thumbs on either side of the opening and she held her breath.

"I think you've been sadly misinformed, little soldier," he said in her ear. "It is not my people trying to conquer your lands. It is the other way around."

What? Why was he mentioning that now? Her shoulders tensed up. She didn't want to think about the conflict between their worlds. They were simply one man and one woman who were about to enjoy the pleasure of each other's bodies.

She felt him step back. Assuming he was unlacing his

breeches behind her, she let the fabric of the dress slide down her arms. When it puddled at her feet, she turned to face him. She was shocked to see him on the other side of the room.

"Good night, Neyla."

Good night? She stood there, blinking. He was leaving? But why?

A sudden hollowness materialized in her stomach, as if she hadn't eaten in days. Crossing her arms over her chest, she tried to think of something to say to get him to change his mind.

But before she could, he was gone, and the sound of the closing door sliced straight through her heart.

CHAPTER SEVEN

Although the village of Greenway was smaller than Crestenfahl, the market had to be ten times larger. Dozens of vendors lined each of the narrow, twisting streets—walkways, really, that spun off from the main square—selling everything from spices and handwoven baskets to earthenware bowls and colorful carpets. The scents of cinnamon and lavender filled the air, along with others Neyla couldn't identify. A person could get really lost if they didn't know where they were going.

A number of people stared at her as she and Rickert strolled through the market. Though she wasn't the only blonde here, she definitely stood out in the sea of dark hair. She wished she was wearing something other than this long dress. Then maybe she'd feel more like herself. She'd borrowed it from Petra, but next time she'd borrow pants.

Or maybe she'd make her own. Yes, that's what she'd do. They were here to visit fabric vendors, after all. Depending on what they had, maybe she'd pick out a few yards and start sewing as soon as they got back.

It wasn't like she had much else to keep herself busy.

She'd done some work with the horses down at the barn until Mr. Riley chased her away. She would've loved to learn some of their hand-stitching techniques, but the older women weren't interested in having her join their sewing circle. Although a few of the younger women, including the very pregnant Petra, told her not to pay any attention to "those crabby old ladies" and to join them anyway, Neyla politely declined, not wanting to make any enemies. One of Lord Tierney's teenage sons had even asked if she'd like to practice shooting a bow and arrow, which had interested her as well, but if the truth came out about her, it might not sit well that she had been wielding a weapon here.

She gave Rickert a sidelong glance. He had an air of quiet confidence and strength about him. He'd been scarce lately, so she relished this one-on-one time with him now.

From her room, she'd seen him a few times down in the courtyard early in the morning, where he led training exercises with some of the young men. According to Petra, the Iron Guild looked for the best and brightest to join their band of warriors. At the festival this summer, there'd be a tryout of sorts, where interested males could show off their skills. She'd enjoyed watching Rickert's half-naked body glistening with sweat as he demonstrated various techniques with the swords he kept on his back.

But as for being alone with him, he'd all but disappeared after that night in her room, and she'd resigned herself to the fact that he was uncomfortable with how close they'd come to making love. He had managed to question her about troop movements and plans a few times, but without her handheld device, she couldn't point out anything on a map. It was depressing how reliant on technology she was. Without it, she basically knew nothing.

"Right this way," he said to her, indicating a row of market stalls.

"Okay." She let her gaze linger on him a moment.

Today, he wore leather breeches and a loose-fitting muslin tunic that somehow managed to accentuate his muscular arms and chest. The white fabric contrasted nicely with his tanned olive skin. His over-the-calf deer-skin boots looked soft enough to sleep in. Criss-crossed over his back was the ever-present weapons belt holding his finely made swords—hand-forged in the fires of Balkirk, he'd told her earlier.

She loved that everything over here was made by hand. It was an art in her world that was long gone. No one she knew knit, cross-stitched, or crocheted anymore—a fact her father had often pointed out.

This morning, when Rickert asked if she'd like to go to Greenway to check out the cloth merchants, she'd jumped at the chance to be with him again.

The mission on the other side would be finished soon, and when it was, Rickert planned to petition the courts to send her home. According to Petra, the magistrate was a former lover of his. If he got his way, which she'd have to imagine was likely, Neyla would soon be gone.

Thinking about that now made her oddly sick inside. Not only would her fate be in the hands of a woman he had once loved, but she and Rickert would soon be parted.

Despite the fact that they were sworn enemies, he struck a chord in her that she couldn't deny. It was as if he knew her better than she knew herself. When she'd opened up to him about her business, he'd been genuinely interested, asking her questions that only someone who cared would ask. He'd validated her feelings and empathized with her as if he knew exactly what she'd been through when she had to sell the shop.

It was crazy, but...she would miss him.

Rickert marched through the market like a man with a mission. Finally, on the next row, he stopped to talk to a merchant. Although Neyla was in good shape from her daily army exercise routine, she was grateful for the break. Now, she could actually look around.

The smell of onions and garlic filled the air. A food vendor stirring a pot flashed her a big grin, his missing front tooth making him look like a Jack o' Lantern. She smiled back at him.

The booth next door was filled with cages of chattering birds. Songbirds mostly, but inside, two large ravens perched on a wooden dowel and watched her with obsidian eyes. For some reason, they made her nervous, so she moved on.

The vendor booth Rickert had stopped at actually belonged to a blacksmith. He was dickering with a soot-covered man about a knife he wanted to buy. Clearly, this was a negotiation that had begun some time ago. She'd have waited, but a display of colorful rugs at another shop drew her attention. The indigos, violets, and tangerines could've come straight out of a bustling Marrakesh plaza and not a medieval market on the far side of an Iron Portal.

"A half-groat to read yer fortune, miss." A man with milky white eyes smiled at her. Glass balls, like the candleholders in Rickert's chambers, sat on his table, and a small golden-haired dog was curled at his feet.

"Is this Esmeralda glass?" She was about to reach for one, but realized she had no money to pay him. Maybe Rickert could—

"Go back where you belong, seasider," a man's voice called out.

She turned to see six or seven men standing in the doorway of what was clearly a hookah bar, given the image on the iron sign out front. Smoke shot from the tallest man's nostrils in twin streams like a dragon's.

"Aye, baby-snatcher. Can't ye figure out how to make yer own? Is that why ye want ours?"

Unease began carving out a pit in her stomach. She looked for Rickert behind her, but didn't see him. Where the hell was he? In fact, where was the blacksmith's shop? It should've been next to the rug merchant's booth, but she couldn't see that, either. Had she wandered farther than she thought? Even the man with the Esmeralda glass was gone.

"I can show the lass how it's done," Dragon-Breath said, stepping off the wooden porch and heading straight toward her, unbuckling his belt. "I've had me a lot of practice."

This was ridiculous. It was broad daylight, for chrissake. And in the middle of town. But as she backed away, the vendors began retreating into their shops and a few of them pulled their shutters closed. The street suddenly seemed narrower, claustrophobic, the sky a thin blue line between the rooftops above her.

Her hand went instinctively for her nonexistent gun. Damn. If this man truly planned to harm her, she could use her Protection-Talent...but if she did, her true identity would surely come out. Besides, any hand-to-hand combat would be next to impossible in this dress.

As she turned to run, a hand reached out to stop her. She was about to clock the guy when she realized it was

Rickert. His eyes blazed with a fury she'd never seen before, his eyebrows two dark slashes above them.

"Back the fuck away," he growled to Dragon-Breath.

"Who's the woman, D'Angelus?"

Rickert stiffened. "None of your bloody business, McCready."

Another man stepped off the porch to join his friend. "Unlike Crestenfahl, we don't allow Pacificans to just walk our streets, mate."

"Aye," Dragon-Breath agreed. "We kill 'em."

"You boys better damn well shut your piss holes or I'll shut them for you." Rickert's voice was low and menacing as he shoved her behind him.

He was protecting *her*? She'd never had this happen before. Even when she'd been mugged a few years ago on the waterfront, her then boyfriend had backed away, leaving her to deal with the situation herself.

"Pretty big words for someone who's outnumbered six to one," Dragon-Breath smirked. "Even if you are in the Guild."

Rickert reached for the hilt of his sword.

"It's okay," she whispered. "We can leave." She didn't want any bloodshed on her account.

She heard the metallic sound of several blades being drawn, but the moment she grabbed Rickert's free hand to pull him away, a warm electrical charge moved up her arm. In an instant, it spread throughout her body and she dropped to her knees, still clutching him.

A gasp went through the small crowd of onlookers and several of the men cried out. She looked up to see an empty bench skitter in the doorway. The wrought-iron sign began swaying on its chain. A sawed-off log seat tipped over and—

"It's levitating!" a woman's voice shrieked.

"Sweet Mother of the Fates," someone else cried.

All of the men fell away and scattered, disappearing into the market without a backward glance. Except for the squeaking sound the sign was making, everything was silent, as if the market were collectively holding its breath.

"Rickert," she said breathlessly. "Oh my God."

The tingling sensation in her arm lessened and the log fell to the ground with a crash. The sound seemed to snap him back to awareness, because he wasted no time pulling her to her feet.

A piece of hair had fallen over his forehead, covering one eye. Combined with the hard set of his jaw and his slightly flared nostrils, he looked wild, like a caged animal ready to attack. He scanned the few onlookers, daring someone else to confront him. When no one did, he scooped her into his arms, plowed through the market without saying a word, and in minutes they were back on his horse.

Her heart thumped loudly in her chest as his

powerful arms encased her, his body almost engulfing hers. When he placed his hands atop hers and positioned them in Duag's long mane to give her something to hold, she felt like a puppet, willing to do anything if he pulled the right string.

"Rickert, what happened back there? Are you all right?"

"Don't know. Don't care." He urged the horse into a gallop.

Her skirts billowed around her legs and her hair whipped across her face as they practically flew down the dirt road. Duag's hooves barely touched the ground.

What was the urgency? Was there some danger she didn't know about…or was it something else? "Where are you taking me?"

His breath was hot against her ear. "Back to Castle Crestenfahl. If I can last that long..."

What was he talking about? As his hips moved with the animal's gait, she noticed the hard ridge of his erection at her back.

Was he—?

Were they going to—?

A wickedly delicious sensation numbed her fingers and toes, tingling between her legs where her body made contact with the saddle. He was going to make love to her when they got back to the castle, she realized with a thrill. She was acutely aware of the leather rubbing her over and over in an erotic rhythm.

Oh God, if she wasn't careful, she could easily have an orgasm right here. Right now.

Don't, Neyla. This is silly. You're on a horse, for God's sake.

His arms tightened around her as if he sensed this argument she was having with her common sense. She arched her neck slightly, wishing they weren't bouncing around so much that she could kiss the tender triangle of skin under his chin.

"You were amazing back there," she told him. "I've never seen anything like it."

His knuckles turned white as he gripped the reins. "Those men—"

"It's okay," she murmured, trying to calm him down. "I'm an outsider. I understand. It's over now."

Instantly, his big hand came up to cup her breast as if claiming her, and he nuzzled the back of her neck. "Aye, it is. You're mine, Neyla, and I'm going to have you now."

Have her? Could he really be this bold and domineering? Clearly, he was unafraid to stake his claim and take what he wanted.

And what he wanted was her.

Excitement prickled along every nerve ending and an aching, almost painful need formed low in her belly.

"If that's a problem," he growled in her ear, "tell me

now, and I'll do what I can to control myself. But if you wait till we get there, it'll be too late."

"I...I want the same thing, Rickert. I want...you."

The incredible sensation between her legs intensified. She realized her hips were grinding her sex against the leather saddle, the thin fabric of her undergarments offering little buffer. As if sensing this, he reached a finger down inside her low-cut bodice and rubbed her aroused nipple. Shards of electricity shot into every corner of her body.

"I plan to get my fill of you. Over and over. So you'd best accept that now, lass."

Oh God, it felt so good. *He* felt so good. She was close. So very close.

She molded herself more tightly against him and let his erection jam against her backside, a promise of what awaited her when they arrived. Although the trees were a blur on either side, she wished Duag could gallop faster. Imagining Rickert's thick shaft greedily pushing its way into her body, filling her to the brink, she could hardly wait.

It would be incredible, of that she was certain. He'd be a masterful, commanding lover. He'd take what he wanted from her and wouldn't be gentle, but she had a feeling it'd be exactly what she'd need.

As if she were inside some magical dream rather than on the back of a horse, her world began to spin around her, taking them higher and higher.

His hand on her breast, pinching, twisting, just to the point of pain. Her core aching from the hard, rhythmic pressure. A gathering, low in her belly.

Until...until...

She stifled a scream as she came.

* * *

The sound of his boots echoed off the stone walls, punctuating his haste to get her to his bedchamber before he exploded. He had barely contained himself the other night when he had helped her with her gown, the only thing stopping him being her obvious reluctance. She'd stiffened when he placed his hands on her. Oh God, he had wanted her that night. Only through extreme force of will had he been able to leave without bedding her.

Praise the Fates, for he sensed an eagerness from her now. A raw, almost palpable energy. Like the anticipation in the air right before a thunderstorm. And if he wasn't mistaken, she'd actually climaxed on the ride here. Without any penetration. Which meant she was very sexually responsive to him. He loved that. A lot. It opened up a whole world of possibilities.

A few people eyeballed them as he carried Neyla through the Great Hall. Someone—maybe Tierney—

chuckled. He took the stairs two at a time and kicked open the door with a bang. With her in his arms, he'd never been more powerful, as though he were twice the man he had been before.

"You do things to me, Neyla. Things I do not understand." He set her down next to the bed. Her hands lingered on his shoulders for a moment before she took a step backwards. He bulged against the leather stretched tightly across his crotch, the heat of her stare electrifying him. "What I do know is that I'm going to take you. Right here, right now, before I lose my mind."

He heard her sharp intake of breath as he unlaced his breeches, springing free his heavy erection. He didn't bother to strip them all the way off. He could do that later.

Why wasn't she naked for him yet? "Your clothing—remove it." He was vaguely aware that he'd said these same words to her before, but under very different circumstances.

She took another step backward and her fingertips grazed the bed, but she didn't immediately comply. "Now," he demanded. "Unless you want me to do it for you."

"I'm capable of undressing myself, Rickert," she said, in that sassy, teasing tone. She grabbed the ties of her riding cape and let it drop to the floor. Her breasts strained at the top of her bodice as she reached around to unfasten it.

Too slow. He grabbed her hands and a rush of energy spread through his body, just as it had at the market. Concentrating on the buttons at the back of her dress, he heard a sound like popping corn as threads broke and the pearls hit the floor.

"Rickert," she said laughing. "This is Petra's dress."

"I'll buy her a new one."

His breath lodged in his throat as he stared at her now naked body. He'd seen a glimpse of her back at the portal, but this time she didn't cover herself from his curious eyes; she stood before him, stroking her fingertips along the muscles of his arms, coaxing him to continue.

"Neyla...Neyla. You are so stunningly beautiful." He could barely form the words with such heady emotion coursing through his veins—the same feelings he'd had with the visions.

If he wanted his life to stay the same, he knew he should stop. Walk away from her again, like he had before. But as her green eyes sparkled with anticipation, and her lips parted, he knew he wouldn't be able to stop now. He was falling for her, and very aware that he was quite possibly looking at his future.

He touched her breasts and she trembled, her pale pink nipples peaking further. He'd been caressing the right one on the ride over, so he now he lavished attention on the left, dipping his head and pulling the nipple into his mouth.

She gasped as she threaded her fingers in his hair. With a patience he didn't know he possessed, he ran his fingers along the length of her hips as he suckled, and the sweet scent of her arousal filled his nostrils.

"Oh...my...Rickert."

Hearing her utter his name like that, intoxicated him further, and he had to possess her. To mark her as his.

With his boots still on and his breeches around his ankles, he pushed her onto the quilts, caging her between his arms. As her cool hands slipped over his hips, he sought out her mouth, vaguely recalling that first beautiful vision he'd seen. The intense lovemaking. The baby-making. However, the gown she wore today was pale yellow, not the blue one from the mist.

No need to think about that now.

This was about sex. Pure, animalistic passion.

With a finger, he parted her folds. She was silky and hot, but her inner walls gripped him tightly. He'd have to go slowly to make sure she could accommodate him. He was large and didn't want to risk hurting her.

His thumb caressed her tender ball of flesh as he slipped a second finger inside. She arched her back and let out a little moan, her muscles clenching around him. Was the lass coming already? Again?

A low growl rumbled in his chest at her hair-trigger

response to him. More of her silkiness coated his fingers.

No, his inner voice shouted. *This one belongs to you. She takes her pleasure as you take yours.*

Withdrawing his hand, he wrapped his fingers around the base of his shaft and positioned himself. The tip slid a little too eagerly along her inner thigh and didn't immediately find her opening. He had to readjust himself and— Ah, there she was.

She was silky and hot, and felt so good around him.

Careful. Slowly.

He gripped the bedclothes in an effort to keep from pushing in too quickly. He could feel the cords in his neck straining. Pausing to give her body a chance to get used to him, he nuzzled her earlobe, kissed her again and, there, she softened a little more.

Five inches. Then six.

She hissed into his ear and he hesitated.

"Are you okay, lass?" He propped himself up to see her face. Her cheeks were flushed, her pupils dilated, but it didn't look like she was in pain.

"Yes," she said simply. "You are...incredible."

He leaned down again and buried his nose in her hair. It smelled like heatherwood.

Seven inches. Eight.

He was going to stop where he always did, thinking she wouldn't be able to take any more of him. Frankly, he was surprised he'd been able to go this far. She was petite and he…wasn't.

"You feel so good, Neyla." He found her lips again and kissed her.

This woman is…is…

Incredibly, she'd softened a little more.

One more steady push and—

There. He was completely inside.

Mine. Neyla, you are mine.

* * *

Rickert's flesh inside her overwhelmed every sense. As his heavy erection rubbed along her sensitive clit, waves of pleasure shot outward. She'd climaxed before he was all the way in and here she was, on the verge again. She might die, he felt that good. He was thick, overpowering, all-encompassing.

Low moans escaped her lips, and if she wasn't careful, they could easily turn into screams.

He stilled. "You're sure I'm not hurting you?" Concern creased his forehead and he brushed a strand of hair from her face.

"This is— You are—" She could hardly compose a coherent sentence. "I'm just trying not to make too much noise." She gave his behind a light slap. "Keep going."

He laughed at her impatience. “Don’t try to keep it bottled up inside, lass. I want you to lose control with me.”

“My control is long gone, Rickert, but I don’t want everyone else to hear us. The windows are open. The courtyard is filled with people.”

More slowly than when he pushed in, he withdrew until he almost broke their connection, his arms and shoulders bulging on either side of her head.

He looked down at her, the blue of his eyes as intense and endless as an arctic sea. “Aye. That is my intention. I want them to know you are mine. ’Tis what we do here. I want them to hear the pleasure I’m giving you.”

Before she could ponder that further, he drove into her again, banishing everything else from her mind. The friction of their bodies felt so incredible that tears stung the back of her eyes. She was coming again.

As if on cue, his shaft seemed to thicken. With a rumbling shout of ecstasy, he gave two quick thrusts, then released himself into her. A noise she didn’t recognize touched the edge of her consciousness. It took her a moment to realize it came from her lips. Had she cried out his name as she climaxed? Had everyone outside heard them?

They stayed joined for a few minutes, every one of her nerve endings ragged and raw, and he slowly softened inside her. Kicking off the breeches that were still around his ankles, he made a move to pull out, but she held him in place.

"I want to sleep with you inside me."

He chuckled. "I'm not sure that's possible, little soldier."

Little soldier? He'd called her that before, she knew, but in this context it was...endearing. Just like when he called her *lass.* It was sexy. She liked it. A lot.

"I'm too heavy," he continued. "You're too small. I'd crush you the minute I fell asleep. Here—" He rolled to his back, bringing her to rest on top of his chest, still not breaking their connection. "How's this?"

"Mmmm, yes." *Perfect.*

With her body draped over him, every muscle spent, his heart beat a steady rhythm beneath her cheek. And as she drifted off to sleep, she thought she heard him say, "I love you, too, little soldier," but she might have been dreaming by then.

CHAPTER EIGHT

Neyla felt the heat of his stare through her closed eyelids. She yawned and rolled over, nestling deeper under the covers. Slightly sore in all the right places, she wasn't ready to get up just yet. She wanted to replay each detail of their lovemaking, sear it into her memory.

Although Rickert had been domineering and controlling, he seemed to know her body better than she did. Everything he tried, every little movement, had pleasured her beyond anything she'd experienced before. She'd never had a man pick her up like that and carry her to his bed. Okay, it was a little barbaric, but it totally turned her on. In fact, everything about him turned her on. His demanding kisses. The warm, salty taste of him. The smell of his musky maleness. Surely, everyone in the market had heard them, just as he had wished.

A tiny surge of dampness tickled her inner thigh. She wanted him again.

"I can tell you're awake, lass. Don't try to pretend you're not."

She groaned from under the covers, delaying the inevitable. She could stay tucked in these sumptuous quilts all day. "I'm still tired."

"Then I guess I'll take this back to the kitchen. Cook will be disappointed."

Food? Her stomach growled and she realized how hungry she was. Starving, in fact. Stretching like a cat, she opened her eyes.

Holy crap. Rickert stood over her, holding a tray of food and wearing only a pair of leather breeches laced loosely up the front. Her hands ached to touch his muscular, well-defined chest and comb through his tousled dark hair. The guy was a freaking olive-skinned Adonis.

Rickert went to the kitchen looking like this? Other women in the castle had seen him...like this? A brief but sudden possessiveness came over her, not unlike when she used her Protection-Talent. Part of her wanted to shield him from others, keep him all to herself.

Rickert sat next to her, a smirk tugging at the corners of his mouth.

"What's so funny?" Was what she'd been thinking so obvious?

"Nothing, lass. Hungry?"

"Famished." She leaned over and gave him a quick kiss on the cheek as he spread jam on a thick, flaky biscuit. "Thank you. And not just for bringing me breakfast."

"Last night was fun, no?" There was that devilish

smile again. It shot quivers of desire straight to her center. "Eat up, because when you're done, I intend to do it all again."

"You...do?"

"Yes. I haven't had my fill of you," he said casually, not looking up from his task. "And given how you responded to me, I'd have to assume the same is true for you."

"Responded?" She was so taken aback by his matter-of-fact tone, she wasn't sure what to say. Yet again, this man had knocked her off-guard.

"You're a very sexually responsive woman, Neyla. I wasn't expecting that."

I am? But then she remembered how many times he'd brought her to climax. What did he mean, he hadn't been expecting that? She'd have to imagine that the other women he'd been with had experienced the same thing. They had to have. How could they not? Sex with this man was...beyond exhilarating.

"In case you didn't know, we men are simple folk. Pleasuring a woman easily, like I clearly did for you last night, is very affirming for us."

She'd never really considered that before. "It's good for your ego?"

He quirked up a brow. "Ego?"

Maybe he wasn't familiar with the word. "Your sense of self. Your manliness."

"Aye. When a woman comes off so quickly, a man feels powerful and strong."

That sounded so primitive, so barbaric. And it totally turned her on.

He held the biscuit impatiently in front of her. "Here. Take it. You need to eat. I wasn't sure what you'd want, so I brought a little of everything."

She could get used to being pampered like this. "Thanks." She took a bite and— Oh God, it was delicious. The pastry was buttery and tender, almost melting in her mouth. The preserves were made of raspberries and another fruit—maybe mango? Wait. Probably *ogappa.*

Rickert didn't take nearly as much care with his own. He quickly slathered another biscuit with jam and stuffed the whole thing into his mouth in one bite. As they ate, she thought about how well she'd been sleeping. It occurred to her that she hadn't had a nightmare about the train accident since coming through the Iron Portal. She would've thought she'd be having all sorts of terrible dreams over here, but she felt wonderfully refreshed and relaxed for the first time in—geez, she couldn't even remember. Even after that stressful incident at the market. Which reminded her…

"What did that guy in Greenway mean when he called me a baby-snatcher?"

The butter knife Rickert was holding fell to the tray. "They're idiots."

"But that's not a normal insult." She took another bite, licking the jam from her finger. "I thought I heard someone say the same thing in one of the shops, too. What does it mean?" It had to be slang for something, or an old wives' tale. They did have some strange terminology here.

He grabbed one of the small silver chalices on the tray and took a long drink. "How did you discover you had a Talent?" he asked, clearly trying to change the subject.

She thought about insisting he continue the conversation, but she knew men well enough to know that he'd be more likely to open up to her once his belly was full. She'd press him later.

"Wait," she said, recalling his stunned reaction in the market and their brief conversation on the ride home. "You had no idea you were a Telekinetic-Talent until yesterday, did you?"

A tiny muscle in his jaw twitched. "No."

"But what about igniting the torches in the portal tunnels?"

"That's nothing special. If I concentrate hard enough, I can make something spark. I've done that all my life. But the market..."

He made a move to stand, but she stopped him with a

hand on his shoulder. She knew firsthand how strange it was to discover you had a latent Talent.

She had a million questions for him. "How old were you when—?"

"I don't want to talk about me," he said quietly. "I want to know all there is about you, Neyla. Your family, your friends, your life."

How was it that this incredibly powerful and sexy man wanted to focus on her, rather than himself? Most men like him had egos the size of Texas. She didn't want to think about her life on the other side. Instead, she wanted to pretend this was her life. A life where she and Rickert were together.

"It's important to me," he said, evidently sensing her reluctance. "Tell me how you discovered you were a Talent."

She sighed. Whatever Rickert wanted from her, she knew she'd eventually comply. But it wasn't because he was strong and she was weak. It was because she wanted to please him, to do what made him happy.

Her thoughts went back to that cold winter morning. It had rained and everyone was wearing hooded Gore-Tex jackets or holding dripping umbrellas.

"I was running late for a meeting," she told him. "Mom had called earlier, saying Dad was sick again and that she was taking him to the clinic. I was going to cancel my appointment, but she insisted I just meet them at the hospital when I was done."

"What kind of meeting couldn't be canceled when a family member is in trouble?"

Clearly, he placed a big emphasis on anything family-related. And he was right. She should've been there. If she had been…

"It was the final gown fitting for an important client's wedding the next weekend, and Mom knew how hard I'd been working on it. All the bridesmaids would be there. It wasn't like Dad hadn't been sick before. I got on the train and planned to wrap things up as quickly as possible, then head to the hospital. We were just pulling into the station…when the Cascadian bombs exploded."

She closed her eyes, still hearing the crunching, screeching metal and all the screams, as if it had happened yesterday. "Although the railcar flipped and landed upside down on the platform, no one inside was badly injured. In fact, ours was the only one in the front half of the train to have any survivors. The authorities suspected someone riding in the car was a latent Protection-Talent who instinctively ran an aura of protection around everyone. After a few tests, they discovered it was me."

When Rickert didn't respond right away, she glanced over. Though his mouth hung open in shock, it didn't surprise her. Most people found the story hard to believe. *She* found it hard to believe, especially since she didn't recall doing anything special at the time. She had been screaming just like the rest of them, hoping and praying she wasn't going to die.

"Cascadian bombs? My people?" His tone was quiet, yet as dangerous as his assassin's knives. "You think we're responsible for a train explosion that killed innocent people?"

This wasn't the reaction she'd been expecting. "Well, uh..."

"I'm in charge of all of the raid operations through this portal, and blowing up trains isn't part of the plan."

"But your people," she protested. "You're fierce fighters. I've seen them."

"Yes, but we kill only Pacifican soldiers when they're searching for entry into our world—because we know what they do when they find one." A shadow fell across his features, making something shift inside her chest. Tightening, squeezing till it almost hurt. "We don't kill innocent people, Neyla. We just don't."

And then she knew. Why else would he risk his life leading team after team through the portals and be gone from his home for months at a time?

"What...what happened to her?" she whispered.

"Who?" It was almost a growl.

She glanced at the ever-present cord around his wrist. "The woman in your locket. Maris."

He exhaled slowly, the tiny muscle in his jaw

twitching, but he said nothing.

Did it hurt too much to explain what had happened to a woman he loved? She touched his arm and tried again. "Please, Rickert. I...I'd like to know. She must've been a very special person. What did they—my people—do?"

"Your people?" His bitter laugh surprised her. She was taken aback for a moment. "Believe me. You're nothing like them."

"But I'm—"

"No," he repeated, looking her straight in the eye. "You're not."

For several long moments he said nothing else, his intense gaze flickering across her features as if he were searching for something within her. Her body felt jittery, jumpy. She wanted him to find what he was looking for. She wanted to be what he needed.

When he finally spoke again, his tone had softened. "I'll tell you, but Neyla, they are *not* your people." He gave her arm a little jerk, emphasizing his point. "It sickens me to hear you say that."

She thought about the army. Indeed, she was a fish out of water there, trying to find her place yet never feeling as if she quite fit in.

"Okay, you're right," she said, stroking a hand over his chest. Touching him seemed to ground her, to clear her mind. "Those are not my people. You...you're my people." There. She'd said it. And it felt so right. So true. Although not everyone had accepted her, she did feel more at home here with him than on the other side without him.

He hesitated, as if he were wondering whether he'd heard her correctly. Then he leaned over the food tray and kissed her. Slowly, tenderly, his mouth undemanding on hers. In this world so different from her own, the pieces of her disjointed life were knitting back into place.

Assuming he wanted to make love again, that the rest of this conversation would have to continue another time, she set the tray aside and reached for him beneath the quilts. He was almost fully erect. Good. She wanted him inside her again.

He gently pushed her hand away. "No. We talk first. I want to tell you about the locket." He unwrapped the necklace from his wrist, carefully setting it on his night table. Then he lay back on the pillow and pulled her with him. "Several years ago, Pacificans discovered a portal we didn't know existed. They crossed through and raided one of our villages."

She'd never heard of Pacificans coming *into* Cascadia. "Raided? Why would they do that?"

His arm tightened around her and he cleared his throat. "They killed almost everyone that day, including my sister, Maris. I...I don't want to forget her or why I'm fighting. Ever. Keeping the locket near keeps my focus on the reason I do what I do. I carry it everywhere and leave it only when I go through the portal."

She glanced at the necklace as her mind swirled with all this new information. Wow. Maris was his sister, not a former lover or wife. But one thing was abundantly clear—Rickert was relentless in his fight for justice for his family. He'd dedicated his life to it. He was a more noble and honorable man than she'd first imagined.

She rubbed her hand over his muscular chest, wishing she could take away his pain. "You said *almost* everyone. A few survived?"

"My nephew Kel."

It felt as if someone had punched her in the gut, and her hands started to shake. Little Kel was his nephew? She recalled the boy Rickert had picked up in the main hall when they'd arrived at the castle. She'd played with him a number of times in the village square. He was a sweet little boy, all smiles and very animated, although she'd never heard him speak a word. She'd even asked Petra about it, wondering if the boy was deaf, and she was told only that something traumatic had happened to him as an infant. "My God, he's only four or five years old, isn't he? He...he survived the raid?"

Rickert nodded.

"But how?"

"He was an infant at my sister's breast when the

raiders stormed the village. I found him crying, hidden in a basket of fabric scraps."

Her breath came in panting gasps and she began to feel lightheaded. Maris must've had enough warning to know they were in grave danger. Neyla couldn't imagine what the woman must've felt, knowing she was going to die but doing what she could in an attempt to save her son.

She didn't want to ask him to tell her more—it was obviously very difficult for him—but she had to hear what happened. She had to know the truth. "Hidden? Because they would have...killed him, too?"

"No," he said flatly.

Her head snapped up. Had she not understood him correctly?

Sounds from the courtyard filtered through the shuttered window. Children laughing. A horse whinnying. Several men arguing about a broken hookah pipe. Funny how the outside world could continue on and be so normal when her own world was falling apart.

For a long moment, he stared at the ceiling, the muscle in his jaw flexing. "The Pacificans come to our villages looking for babies."

The sudden lump in her throat made it nearly impossible to breathe. "Babies? But...but why? I don't understand."

"To steal them."

A dull roar sounded in her head, drowning out his voice. The man at the market. He'd called her a baby-snatcher.

"Some say our children are the most beautiful," Rickert was saying. "Smarter. Stronger. Healthier. Lots of reasons have been bandied about as to why they want them. Some even say they eat them."

"Eat?" Bile rose in her throat. Oh God, she was going to be sick.

"No one really believes that, Neyla, but we all grew up with the songs."

"Songs?"

"I think you call them nursery rhymes." He flashed an impish smile. Grateful, she recognized it as his way of lightening up the heavy atmosphere. Then he cleared his throat and began to sing. She was stunned at how beautiful his voice was. Although it was a child's melody, his tone was rich and deep. How strange that an assassin could sing like an angel.

Would he ever stop surprising her?

When he finished, it dawned on her that she hadn't been paying attention to the lyrics. "Sing it again. I'm afraid I wasn't listening to the words."

He sang it slower this time.

Run, ye lads and lasses, for the devil's men draw near.
Wi' hungry maws and blackened hearts

The end is almost here.

They cut ye wi' a knife and fork and sprinkle ye wi' sollet.

One. Two. Three. Four.

Ye're down the devil's gullet.

She knew most nursery rhymes contained an element of truth and that many were quite macabre. "That's about...Pacificans?" She'd almost said *us*. "They're the devil's men?"

"The truth is, although most of the old magic of our world is gone, it still resides in some of us." He patted his chest. "There are those in your world who want it and that's why they come here to get it. They want the power—our power—to defeat us and expand their control in your world."

She tried to follow what he was saying. "Magic resides in you? You mean, people with Talents?"

"Yes. Not all of us have them, but Pacificans breach the portals to take our children, hoping that some of them have the *fata* blood in their veins."

"*Fata?*"

"We are an ancient race of people, descended from the Fates, and our world once held a very powerful magic." He glanced at her quizzically. "Are you sure you don't know this?"

She shook her head. It sounded like Celtic lore, not real life.

"Three brothers, two born with powers and one without, controlled the three kingdoms. A power struggle, stemming from jealousy and greed, where one brother wanted what the other ones had, started the Obsidian Wars. The Fates finally had to step in and create the separate worlds."

"And where does the baby snatching come in?"

"If they take our children who have it inside them, they can use them to their advantage."

She had grown up in a world of technology and computers, not magic and kingdoms. And yet...

Her thoughts spun with all this new— "Oh my God. The hospital ward."

"What?"

"All recruits are required to get mandatory birth control injections in case...in case..."

"In case what?" he coaxed.

"In case the barbarians—I'm sorry, Rickert—overtake us in the field."

Neyla recalled when she got her first birth control shot as part of her induction into the army. They'd been told that Cascadians were no better than the marauding Vikings had been centuries ago, raping innocent women and fathering bastard children. During orientation, they'd watched a heart-wrenching video about a woman who'd been assaulted by a Cascadian raider. She'd given birth to a child that she gave up for adoption.

"I was late for my appointment at the women's health center, and I got lost in the hospital." The unmarked corridors were so confusing. "Somehow, I ended up in front of a nursery. I peered through the glass to see a half dozen or so swaddled infants. Some were crying. Others were sleeping. All of them had small white cards taped to their clear plastic cribs, with a single number written in black ink, no names. Baby number three, a little boy—well, I assumed he was a boy because he was wrapped in a blue flannel blanket—was sucking his thumb, just staring at me."

Something about the place had seemed off, she recalled. Maybe it was the drab, grey tiled room. Or the absence of any smiling parents. Or the heavyset nurse propping bottles in the cribs to feed the babies rather than cradling them in her arms. For some reason, those disturbing images had reminded Neyla of photos she'd seen of Romanian and Chinese orphanages. All those babies and no one to love them.

"I wondered if they were the bastard children I'd heard about. I felt sorry for baby number three for being the product of—of a violent man and an innocent woman." She started to falter, but Rickert's hand covered hers, urging her to continue. "I heard something behind me and turned around."

She told him about the two nurses coming out of a door she hadn't noticed before.

"Are you an applicant?" the first woman had asked. She wore her hair in two burrito rolls that framed her pinched face. "Because if you are, you're too early."

"Yeah," the other one said, locking the door behind them. "These foundlings are not being assigned to their families until next month."

"Foundlings?" Neyla hadn't heard that term before. Weren't they...bastard children?

The burrito-hair nurse turned beet red, and Neyla had thought she might strike the other nurse. "You know better than that, you idiot." Turning back to Neyla, she forced a smile. "What she meant was that these unwanted children—bastards, if you will—are going to be ready for adoption next month. Their inoculations and tests will be complete by then, and the first viewings will take place next week. You'll get a chance to hold each one and make your decision at that time. Then the committee will decide where to place each child."

It sounded like the process of adopting a dog from a shelter, not a baby from a hospital. "I'm...I'm..." She hadn't wanted to tell them that she wasn't there to adopt, that she'd simply taken a wrong turn and—

Rickert put his hand on her shoulder, yanking her from her thoughts. "What is it, lass?"

"At the time, I didn't understand what she meant, but they had called them *foundlings*—the babies in the cribs.

Foundlings! Oh my God, they weren't *found* children or bastard children. They were *stolen babies.* Stolen from Cascadia." A cold lick of panic crawled up her spine and settled into her pores. "Wait. How long has this been going on?"

"The snatching of babies?" he asked.

"Yes."

"I don't know. A long time. Why?"

Her vision became blurry, her voice hiccupped in short gasps as she tried to breathe. "My mother used to... She'd tell me bedtime stories. About faeries. And how they'd brought me to her and my father...when I was an infant."

"What are you saying, Neyla?" He held her face in his hands and touched his forehead to hers.

"They were just stories, or so I thought, but I was adopted, Rickert. *Adopted.*" It felt like her head might explode. "Both my brother and I were. I was told that my birth mother was too young to keep me, so she gave me up. But I have Talents, so maybe I'm...I'm..."

Rickert's strong, warm arms encased her, and she smelled the heatherwood soap on his skin. She only knew she was crying when he gently wiped her cheek with a callused thumb. She could hardly comprehend the enormity of it all. Pacificans coming through the portals, killing innocent people and stealing children.

Could she have been born in Cascadia and stolen by

raiders? Were her real parents brutally killed as Kel's had been? She felt as if someone had turned her body inside out, upsetting everything she'd once held to be true.

In the quiet and through her tears, she pieced together what she knew. Rarely were the reports of fighting covered by the non-army news media. Her online friends thought she was paranoid when she talked about the dangers of riding on trains and going to nightclubs and other large gathering places. They'd heard about the train accident, but argued that a derailment had caused the crash, not an explosion by Cascadians. She hadn't believed them…until now.

Add to it Maris's death, babies referred to as *foundlings,* even the nursery rhyme. It all made perfect sense. The army had lied to her. They'd lied to everyone.

"I'm sorry…about your sister and little Kel."

Rickert stroked her hair and held her close. "Shhh," he murmured again and again. "It's okay, lass. It's not your fault. You didn't know. It's possible you were a victim, too."

Overcome by his concern for her, she couldn't seem to stop the tears from falling. She knew that she loved him, but feared she didn't deserve him. She cried for the horrible losses Rickert and Kel had suffered at the hands of those people. And although she hadn't worked for the army back then, she cried for her part in helping them now.

* * *

"Easy, boy," Rickert said, steadying Duag as he pulled back the bowstring. The arrow flew through the air, only to lodge in the trunk of a sapling on the far side of the clearing. The buck they'd been tracking for almost an hour spun and disappeared into the forest. "Bloody hell."

His uncle inclined his head toward the tree. "On account of your woman?" It wasn't often Rickert missed an easy shot.

"Aye," Tierney's youngest son Willem said. "We heard what happened at the market. That you lifted tables and chairs and you threw some men out of the hookah bar without touching them."

"That was unplanned," Rickert admitted to the boy. He chose to ignore Tierney's question.

"You sure gave those McCready boys a new appreciation for the D'Angelus clan indeed," Tierney said. "Reminds me of the tricks your pa used to pull. *Och*, he was a rascally bastard."

"Uncle Carrick was a Talent, too?" Willem asked, wide-eyed.

"Aye. A Fire-Talent, like Rickert."

Rickert snorted. His command over fire was nothing

like his father's had been.

Tierney continued. "Though I never saw him do anything like what I heard you did in Greenway."

Although he was curious about what his uncle had heard, Rickert kept silent, uncomfortable about discussing his Talents just yet. It was too new. Too confusing. And, as he thought about Neyla's part in the whole thing, it was too damned personal. If dozens of people hadn't witnessed the incident, he'd have wondered whether it had really happened.

With a tap of a spur, he cantered Duag to the edge of the forest and retrieved his arrow from the sapling. They continued hunting small game throughout the rest of the afternoon—red-tailed turkeys, rainbow partridges, mountain squirrels—as the deer and wild boar were scarce. Apprehension kept prickling the back of his neck, but he rubbed it away. The forests and glens were usually teeming with bigger game, but not today. Maybe winter was coming earlier this year.

They stopped when they got to a small clearing and Willem twisted in his saddle. "Can you do it now, Rickert? I want to see you move something."

"I can't. I've tried." And he had. Several times.

"There's one now, son," Tierney said, changing the subject. He pointed to a red-tailed turkey under a large *ogappa* tree. "See him?"

"Aye, Papa. I see him." The tip of the boy's tongue

stuck out between his teeth as he took aim with his slingshot.

"That's it. Take a deep breath, then release it."

Just as the boy was ready to shoot, his pony pawed at the ground, jostling him in the saddle and destroying his concentration. "Juju, whoa." When he took aim again, the pony tossed his head. Tears welled up in Willem's eyes and he quickly turned away so his father wouldn't see.

"Here, I'll hold him steady." Rickert reached down and grabbed the bridle. "I had a naughty pony when I was your age, so I know how frustrating they can be. He pulled all sorts of nonsense, hoping to get away with it."

"You did?"

"Aye." He glanced at the cowlick on the pony's face. "Have you noticed the whirl pattern of Juju's white star? It's slightly off-center, no?"

The boy nodded, moisture glittering from the corners of his eyes.

"My pony's star was slightly off-center like that, too. It's the mark of a horse who thinks he's smarter than you are and who will pull all sorts of tricks."

"Then I need a new pony. A horse this time. Like Duag."

"Not so fast," Rickert said, laughing. "Juju will make you a better rider than if you had a perfect pony. You learn to be prepared for anything—and what to do when things go wrong."

Duag started to pin his ears—he did not like another horse this close unless it was a mare in heat—but Rickert gave him a low warning and he stood quietly. The pony didn't move, either.

"Okay, little man, I've got him. Go ahead and try it again."

Fortunately, the turkey was still scratching for bugs at the base of the tree. Willem aimed and took the shot. With a surprised cluck and a flurry of feathers, the bird fell dead.

"Ho-ye," Rickert exclaimed. "Looks like we're having turkey for dinner."

"Excellent shot, son," Tierney said, clapping.

Grinning from ear to ear, Willem leapt from the saddle and ran to retrieve the turkey.

Tierney turned to Rickert. "Thank you for that. He really looks up to you."

"He's a good lad."

Tierney nodded. "That he is. Just think...in a few more years, Kel will be joining us. And after that, one of your own."

Rickert reached down and absently patted Duag's neck. Years. He didn't want to think about the passage of time. It reminded him how little of it he had left with Neyla.

"Listen, Rickert...about your woman."

He jerked his head up, his gaze meeting Tierney's, a surge of pride filling his veins. He liked—loved—that people recognized Neyla as his woman. She was his, and he was hers. At least until she had to leave.

"What about her?" he asked cautiously, narrowing his eyes. Tierney hadn't found out who she was, had he? He quickly dismissed the thought. The man wouldn't be so jovial if he knew how she and Rickert had met. He considered telling Tierney about Neyla's foundling story, but every time he opened his mouth, he stopped. He didn't want to risk her being sent to the jail pits to await trial.

"She's got you all tore up inside, does she?" Tierney laughed. "Don't act so surprised. It's obvious your head's with her and not on hunting."

"I...ah..."

Tierney shifted the thin stick of *ogappa* bark to other side of his mouth and chewed on it thoughtfully. "She holds the key, doesn't she?"

"The key?" Rickert didn't understand.

"As someone with abilities, do you sense the *fata* blood in her? Because strange things can happen when two Talents merge like that. It would explain what happened in the market. A pooling of your magic, if you will. It's possible she doesn't know she has it."

Rickert cringed inwardly. He didn't want to get into any of that now. Protection-Talents were so rare

Tierney would wonder if and how the Pacificans were using her. He wasn't ready for his uncle to know he'd deceived him. At least not yet. Not until he had some sort of plan.

One option he'd briefly considered was for he and Neyla to run away together. Despite the fact that a relationship between them didn't make sense, he'd fallen in love with her. He couldn't bear the thought of being apart from her, let alone seeing her punished for something he'd done.

However, he'd never run from anything in his life. He met challenges head on. And he wasn't willing to give up the fight against those who came through the portals, either. Until he figured out what to do about Neyla, he wanted to put things off as long as he could. But the court would soon be arriving in town, and then he'd have to come clean. Saffira, his former lover, was a *taghta* magistrate. You couldn't exactly lie to a Truth-Seer. He'd tried that before and had learned a hard lesson.

Maybe he should sneak Neyla back through the portal while he still had time, then come back and face his punishment. She'd been raised on the other side and that was all she knew. Life here was much different than it was in Pacifica. Too different. To assume she'd want to stay with him and give up her life there would be selfish. She had a mother and brother who loved her. He wouldn't ask that of her.

"It was a bolt of energy coursing through my system in the market," Rickert said. "I've never felt that before." He left out the part about tearing off her dress and making wild, ravenous love to her later. It had probably just been residual power from what had happened in Greenway.

"Anger and passion are two powerful emotions, Rickert. They're able to stir up all sorts of mischief. Those boys in Greenway were threatening her and you were only—"

"Papa, look."

The two men followed where Willem was pointing.

Rickert was stunned to see Asher staggering out of the trees. His second in command was limping, his leg covered in blood.

"The portal's been breached," Asher called out, leaning on his big dog for support.

Breached? Pacifican murderers were back in Cascadia?

He scanned the forest, but he saw no one else. Where were the rest of his men? He spurred Duag into a gallop. Without slowing, he leaned over and pulled Asher up behind him.

"What happened? Where is everyone?" He thought about Petra's younger brother, Fallon. Konal and Toryn, his weapons experts. Grady, Quaid, Oran… He prayed to the Fates that his men were still alive. If they weren't...

"They're on the other side," Asher choked. "In the northern quadrant, just like we'd planned. The mission was successful, so the men went to celebrate. Before I met up with them, I doubled back and discovered evidence that one of the Pacifican army units may have found the portal location. There wasn't time to round everyone up, so I crossed through on my own. And Rickert," he said, breathing heavily, "they brought guns through the portal."

"Bloody bastards." Rickert absently reached for the locket around his wrist. The raiders who attacked his sister's village had brought guns through the portal as well, sacrificing some of their own men who carried them. "We must mobilize our—"

Asher interrupted. "And I found...Fallon...in the antechamber. Dead."

It felt as if someone had punched Rickert in the gut, forcing all the air from his lungs. Petra's brother was young, with his whole life ahead of him.

"It's my fault," Asher choked out. "I knew he wasn't with the rest of the men, but I assumed he went to hook up with a woman he met earlier."

"Dead?" Young Willem asked, as if the news had just sunk in. "Fallon is dead?"

"Yes," Asher replied soberly. "From the Iron Death. The army must've captured him, then used him to bring the guns through. I managed to kill one of them, but the rest got away."

A cold lick of fury ran down Rickert's spine. He never should've stayed on this side as long as he had. Iron sickness be damned.

"Which way were they headed?" Lord Tierney asked.

"I lost them after they crossed the river. I...I couldn't keep up."

"If they went across the river, that means they were heading away from Crestenfahl," Lord Tierney said, the relief evident in his voice.

But Rickert was far from comforted by this news. His people were still in danger. "Then we need to mobilize the teams back at Crestenfahl and spread out. We're going to hunt down those bastards and kill them."

CHAPTER NINE

Neyla had never been more determined in her life. She took the gelding's reins from the stable boy.

"Please, ma'am. I'm not supposed to let anyone leave. It's too dangerous."

"You're going to open the gate for me. And you're going to open it now!"

Rickert and the rest of the manhunt had left hours ago. Sick with worry, she couldn't possibly wait any longer. Petra's brother had died, and she feared others would die, too. After failing to convince Rickert to take her along, even when she reminded him of her Protection abilities, she resigned herself to staying in Crestenfahl. But she'd waited long enough.

"My father will use a bollock vise on me if I don't obey orders."

She had no idea what that was and didn't care to know. "What if I *made* you open it?"

"Let me talk to Mr. Asher first."

She let out a sound of exasperation. "He smoked some *prath* for the pain when they stitched him up, so he's resting and can't be disturbed. Please, you must open the gate."

"I...I can't."

Fine. Closing her eyes to calm herself, she focused inward and the little hairs on her arms prickled. Hopefully the kid hadn't experienced what it felt like to be surrounded by a ring of protection. From her understanding, it took a little getting used to. Energy rippled off her skin and charged the air around her. When she concentrated it in his direction, he yelped.

"Hellfire!" the boy exclaimed, shaking his arms like a ragdoll and stepping sideways. She moved the shield with him. "All right. I'll open the bloody gates."

* * *

The moon illuminated the thick cloud cover, making it glow an ominous grey-green in the night sky. Exhausted by the breakneck speed of her ride, Neyla reined the gelding to a walk.

Shouldn't she have come to that turnoff by now? She craned her head around. The stable boy had said to veer left at a charred *ogappa* tree, but she hadn't seen one. Had she galloped past it in the dark? Although he didn't seem devious enough, the thought did cross her mind that the young man had given her bogus directions on where Rickert and his men were headed.

An odd smell hung in the air and she sniffed more

deeply. Something was burning, but it wasn't the now-familiar scent of dried cedar and applewood stoking a cooking fire. She urged the gelding forward. Up ahead, an orange light flickered through the trees. When they rounded the corner, she saw Rosamund's cottage—its roof in flames.

Adrenaline shot through her, expelling her fatigue. Leaping off the horse, she ran through the garden gate. The heat was unbearable when she got to the porch. The crackling of the wooden structure was deafening and she backed away. Although she couldn't be permanently injured by fire, it would still hurt.

Please let there be no one inside.

Taking a calming breath, she tried to settle herself again. But when she stretched out her protection ring, she didn't feel any live bodies. Had Rosamund and her daughters gotten out in time?

She thought she saw a shadow moving in the barn. Rosamund? She was about to call out when the woman appeared in the window, her finger to her lips. Neyla didn't understand. What was—?

Something familiar pricked at her senses.

"Trihorn?" a voice called out from behind her. "Is that you?"

Her heartbeat thundered like a thousand hooves behind her eardrums as she spun around.

Gravich and six other soldiers on horseback stood at

the edge of the forest.

"Captain!" she managed to gasp, though her mouth was now bone dry.

The men wore a strange assortment of clothes, probably obtained from the warriors' trunks on this side of the portal. She recognized the horses as coming from Rosamund's barn.

"What happened?" Gravich asked, his ever-present scowl darkening his features. "Were you captured?"

"I...uh...yes."

All of the men, including the Captain, held the reins awkwardly in each hand, hunching their backs in an attempt to protect their balls from the saddle. One of the horses kept tossing its head and she noticed the bridle had been put on backward. It was clear that none of them were familiar with riding.

"And you escaped," he said. "I honestly didn't know you had it in you, Trihorn. Good job. I'll have to recommend you for the extraction team next time. You're clearly ready for it."

"Extraction team?" She'd never heard of such a group. Just what were they planning to...?

It was then that she noticed several of the horses had small metal boxes the size of cat carriers tied behind the saddles, and a terrible knot began to form in her stomach.

Those boxes were the perfect size to hold a baby.

An intense anger heated her veins and burned her cheeks, as if she were on fire like the cottage behind her.

Gravich and his men were planning to steal Cascadian infants. And Petra's brother had died the Iron Death by carrying their guns and these metal cages through the portal. A vital young man—gone.

For the first time since joining the army, she didn't try to stem the hate she felt for this horrible man and his soldiers. Before coming through the Iron Portal, she'd suppressed those feelings, thinking her reaction was wrong because they had such a noble mission...and because, for once, her father had been proud of her.

But no more. Thunder rolled in the distance, as if echoing her indignation, and a few thick raindrops landed on her head.

"As soon as we get back to the other side," Gravich was saying, "I'll recommend you for the program."

She was about to give them a big fat *hell, no,* when she saw one of the soldiers looking toward the barn. Oh God, he hadn't seen Rosamund, had he?

Her gaze darted sideways. She had to act fast.

Think. Think.

She could extend a ring of protection around the woman and her daughters. No, that wouldn't prevent Gravich from grabbing Neyla and removing her from the scene. The shield worked best the closer she was to the subjects. And once she was gone, the women would be vulnerable.

Okay, scratch that idea.

So she did the only other thing she could think of. Grabbing her gelding's reins, she swung into the saddle.

"So where are you headed?" she asked, urging the animal straight toward the man who'd been looking at the barn. His horse swung its hip around in response and pinned his ears.

"Jesus Christ," the man bellowed, grasping the saddle with both hands to keep from falling off. The others laughed.

She needed to distract them, get them away from Rosamund's place, and then she'd worry about what to do next. As soon as she knew the woman and her daughters were safe, she'd be able to think more clearly and figure out how to get away to warn Rickert.

Gravich was still talking. "So how did you get through the portal? We knew you were here, but couldn't figure out how you did it."

Dread sucked at her insides like a vacuum. How the hell had they known she was here?

"I don't understand. How'd you find me? I thought I was...on my own."

Gravich laughed. "You're chipped, Trihorn—all the Talents are. The scar on your upper arm? It's a subcutaneous location device. We just followed the signal."

A wave of nausea rose into her throat and she leaned

heavily on her horse's withers. So she had led the enemy here. She was responsible for what happened to Petra's brother. And to Rosamund's home.

Her fingers tracked up her arm to the raised bit of thickened skin—there it was, just under the surface. She'd been told it was a scar from a vaccine. It took all her willpower not to gouge the thing out with her nails. She should've guessed as much. They microchipped all the canines. Why not the Talents, too?

* * *

"What in the hell were you thinking, Rickert? Or is that the point? You *weren't*?" Big Thom pulled his horse too close to Duag. The stallion would've bit the man or the horse, but Rickert reined him away.

"It's not possible. Neyla is not helping the Pacificans." She wouldn't have betrayed him.

"Are you calling me a liar? There's no doubt what I saw. She was riding with at least half a dozen of them, leading them in the direction of Crestenfahl. They were talking and their leader kept referring to her as Agent Trihorn. I was hiding out in one of the buried mud huts on the side of the river and heard them plain as day. And yes, they do have guns."

Rickert scrubbed a hand through his hair. He'd given the oldest stable boy strict orders not to let Neyla out beyond the castle walls. She had argued vehemently to go with Rickert, saying she could protect him and his men, but he wouldn't allow it. What had happened? If only Asher hadn't been so incapacitated. "They were riding? Where did they get the horses?"

"The chestnut gelding she rode is from the Crestenfahl livery," Big Thom answered. "I'm not sure about the others. One of them had the markings of a horse I've seen at the Guthrie farm."

He drew in a ragged breath. The invaders had been to Rosamund's place. Were the three women still alive? He ground his teeth in an effort to stave off memories of what had been done to his sister's village.

Big Thom continued. "You let your dick get the best of you this time, and now we'll all suffer."

He wanted to beat the bloody hell out of the bastard. "I don't care what you saw. Neyla is not a traitor." She cared deeply for him and his people and would never do anything to jeopardize their safety. He knew that with every fiber of his being. "Willem, get to your father's team and tell him to send someone to the Guthrie farm, then meet us back at Crestenfahl."

Without waiting for the others, he spurred Duag into a gallop.

CHAPTER TEN

Although Neyla was completely turned around and could never have found her way back to Crestenfahl, Gravich knew its rough coordinates based on information they'd recorded from her tracking device. She made them stop a few times, saying her horse had picked up a stone in its hoof, but that hadn't stalled them for long. At dawn they emerged from the forest. The closed gates of the town loomed ahead at the top of the hill.

"Trihorn, you may want to give us a few minutes inside before you bring up the rear." A couple of the soldiers laughed, but when she glared at them to see what was so funny, they refused to meet her gaze.

"Why?"

"Let's just say we have some man-stuff to take care of before we look for anything else."

"You're going to...?" The innocent faces of the people she'd lived with these past few weeks flashed before her eyes. "No. You can't."

"All's fair in love and war," someone said.

"Petroff, goddammit," Gravich barked from the back of his horse. "Give Trihorn the reins, then get your ass over here and start lighting these torches."

"But I'm—"

"Do it now or I'll volunteer you to bring all the iron back through the portal like I did with that barbarian."

Several of the men laughed.

"His name was Fallon," she said angrily. No one seemed to have heard her.

"Decker, Branson, you too." Gravich turned in the saddle. "Trihorn, do you know any other ways in or out of the city? Not sure how effective we'll be setting fire to that gate in this rain, although maybe we can scale it with the equipment we smuggled through the portal."

She shook her head numbly and took the reins from Petroff and the other men. Rickert's acceptance and love for who she was instead of who others claimed she should be, contrasted with these ruthless, depraved soldiers, made her realize that she'd allowed the opinions of others to dictate how she lived her life.

But no longer.

More than likely, she'd been stolen as a baby from her home and carried through a portal by men like these. Men who had probably killed her birth parents. Glancing at the small metal boxes that would be used to transport infants, she knew exactly what she needed do.

"It's now or never," she mumbled to herself as she dismounted. With a few slaps, she turned the horses loose and they galloped into the gloom.

"What the hell? What are you doing?" Petroff's high-pitched voice cracked, a lit torch clutched in his hand.

"For God's sake, Trihorn," Gravich said. "Do you ever think? We need those packs. They have all of our supplies we need to scale these walls. Get those goddamn horses rounded up."

She took a step backward toward the gate. "No."

Gravich turned in his saddle and glared at her. "What do you mean, no? I gave you a direct order, Trihorn, and I expect you to carry it out."

Neyla took a deep breath. "I've actually thought quite a lot over these past few weeks and have made some important realizations. I've put up with your lies, your brutality, for far too long. And for what? So you can come over here and steal children? Rape and murder the villagers? For God's sake, how can you people live with yourselves? Captain, aren't you married? Don't you have children?"

Gravich pulled at the collar of his shirt and she took a few more steps backward. "Leave my personal life out of it. What I do here is of no concern to those on the other side."

"It's not? I'll bet your family would think otherwise." She pointed to everyone. "You all make me sick. You're the barbarians, not them."

She'd never attempted to protect a structure before, but she sure as hell was going to try. The pull of the thick mud made each step difficult as she ran toward the wall. Suddenly, Gravich was in front of her, his horse blocking the way, and she skidded to a halt. She tried to sidestep around the animal, but Gravich reached over and grabbed her.

"Trihorn, don't be so foolish," he said, dismounting without losing his grip on her. "It's a classic case of Stockholm Syndrome. You should remember this from your training. It's when prisoners develop an attachment to their captors. Now, come on. Help us with our mission and we'll take you back to New Seattle where you belong."

"You told me once I needed to be passionate about what I did in order to be successful."

He was huffing and puffing, his round face red and sweaty. "Ah, so you were listening."

Bastard. "Well, I'm passionate about the man I love... and I'm passionate about these people."

Anger-fueled adrenaline surged in her veins. In a blinding fury, she twisted, thrashed and kicked. Something crunched and Gravich cursed.

"Stupid, high-maintenance Talent," he said, falling to the ground. "All of you fucking Talents are."

She didn't look to see what she'd done to him. Instead, she sprinted toward the gatehouse, where she would stretch out a protection ring before someone else got to her. If she could stay away from them, she might be able to hang on until Rickert and his men returned.

In the pale light, she could just make out a few wide-eyed faces peeking out from above the wall. Even though Rickert's second in command was hurt, maybe the powerful warrior could help keep the enemy at bay.

She started to call out for someone to get Asher, when something clamped around both her legs. She went down hard. A heavy body slumped over her, crushing her into the mud and knocking the breath from her lungs. She couldn't move.

"Not fast enough," Gravich snarled.

* * *

Rickert pulled up his horse at the edge of the forest, having left the rest of the group far behind. The southern wall of the city was dark—no flames, no smoke—but something to the right caught his attention. Several horses—fully saddled, packs loaded—grazed in the field opposite Crestenfahl. Two figures scrambled toward them.

His eyes narrowed with hate. Pacifican invaders.

But where the bloody hell was Neyla?

He'd never wanted their technologies before, but he found himself desperately wishing he could contact her through one of those cellular phones. To hear her voice. To know that she was all right. That she was far away from the danger and violence of this war between the realms.

But she wasn't. Unless she'd escaped, she was still in the hands of the enemy.

The thought of her with those bastards drove him nearly mad as he spurred Duag forward.

In the time they'd been together, she'd become an important part of his life. Like his arms. His legs. He couldn't imagine what he would be like without her. That beautiful and spirited young woman had drawn him out of his endless darkness and into the light. It was hard to believe that he'd once considered her his enemy. Because of her, he had a reason to live his life again, not just exist.

Neyla. Lass, where are you?

As if in answer, an energizing heat shot up his forearms, into his torso, and settled in his belly the way it had back at the market.

Thank the Fates. She was nearby.

The road curved, and at the far corner of the walled city, two figures were struggling on the ground. A beast of a man, holding a lit torch, and—

Neyla.

Fury pinpointed Rickert's focus, making the sensations in Greenway seem as mild as tepid bathwater. The woman he loved was in trouble at the hands of an enemy that had destroyed so much already. He urged

Duag faster. The stallion's hooves pounded loudly on the muddy road. He concentrated his anger on her attacker and the torch in Neyla's face flared out. Then the bastard's hair and clothes began to smoke before he flew backward as if struck by an invisible hand.

Leaping from Duag's back, he sprinted toward her.

Neyla yelled something but the air snapped with electricity, drowning out her voice.

He hurled his body to cover hers as the sharp crack of gunfire echoed against the outside of the castle wall. Something thunked against his chest just as he reached her. A bullet? He waited for a burning pain to radiate outward, but all he felt was a dull sting above his heart, like a hit from a slingshot. The only thing that mattered was that Neyla was in his arms, safe and sound.

"Oh my God, are you okay, Rickert?" She grasped at his clothes. "Did Gravich shoot you?"

That was Gravich? Her captain? "Yes, but...your...your shield...it protected me." He buried his face in her wet hair. More shots rang out, but he kept her tucked beneath him.

"Thank God I got it up in time. I didn't see you, but I could feel you. They can't hurt—"

"Shhh," he said. "I'm not letting you go."

"Listen, Rickert. Their guns can't hurt us." She pushed him away. Even covered in mud with her hair whipping across her face in the wind, she was the most beautiful creature he had ever seen. "I'll protect you," she said, kissing him. She tasted of the rain and earth here in Cascadia, and it occurred to him that she was as much a part of this world as he was.

"But—"

"Trust me," she said. "I'll be fine. You need to kill those bastards. They came to steal babies and they laughed about killing Fallon. Please, Rickert. Go. Don't let them get away."

With her protection field surrounding him, Rickert stood and pulled out the Balkirk swords that criss-crossed his back. "I love you," he heard her say as he turned to face the enemy.

Shouts and a barrage of gunfire rang out again. A bullet grazed his shoulder and another his temple, but he felt nothing more than a sting as he advanced on the closest Pacifican soldier. With a hard thrust, he plunged a blade deep into the man's gut, then quickly pulled it out. As the body crumpled to the ground, Rickert turned his attention to the next one and killed him, too. With Neyla's protection ring around him, he felt invincible.

Where was the bastard who had threatened her?

Two shots rang out, and Rickert turned.

Gravich, his clothes blackened and hair singed, had reached one of the horses. Aiming his gun haphazardly at Rickert, he fired again.

Click. Click.

The chamber was empty.

He was going to enjoy ending this man's life, he thought as he strode toward him. No one threatened Neyla and lived.

Gravich threw down the weapon. "Get away from me, you freak."

"Big words from a man who comes into this world to prey on our innocent wee ones."

The soldier untied a small metal cage from the saddle and flung it as Rickert got closer. It deflected off his shoulder and bounced harmlessly to the ground. Printed on the side was the number three, reminding him of Baby Boy Number Three Neyla had seen in the nursery.

"We do not prey on your infants. We remove them from your primitive, medieval world and give them far more opportunities than they can get here."

"You call being stolen from your home a better life? Your parents killed?" He recalled the image of his sister's body and he gripped his weapons tighter. "You are not gods. You are men. Despicable, vile men who care only about the power and might our children may bring you."

On second thought...

He sheathed his swords and withdrew one of his shorter blades. He wanted to see the whites of this man's eyes as he filleted him open, killing him slowly.

"We only take what should be ours." Gravich grabbed at the reins, jerking the horse's head around.

"Why should your people be the only ones with *fata* magic?"

The man managed to climb into the saddle, but before he could settle himself, the horse squealed and jumped sideways.

Duag stood in the space where the mare had been, nostrils flared, tail up. He must've nipped her flank, but the female had wanted nothing to do with him.

Gravich clutched at the saddle, trying to keep his balance, but he slid awkwardly from the animal's back. Instead of hitting the ground, however, his foot caught in the stirrup. And then the mare bolted.

The soldier screamed, a high-pitched sound of panic. Unable to break free, he was dragged like a ragdoll, his head striking the boulders on the muddy road that led to the Iron Portal.

Normally, Rickert would've felt cheated that such a vile enemy of his people hadn't died by his own hand. But for once, he had more important matters to attend to.

CHAPTER ELEVEN

Rickert stood in front of the large, ornately carved mirror on the far side of the room and beckoned to Neyla. He wore a dark robe and had a gleam in his eye that promised all sorts of decadent, naughty, and very delightful pursuits.

With the festivities finally over, she couldn't wait to tumble into bed with him.

"Your gown—it's the one you were wearing in my first vision of us together." His gaze ran over her body like a caress.

Acutely aware of the heat throbbing between her thighs, she wondered why she didn't just strip off her clothes, run over there, and ravish him. Instead, she smoothed a hand over the periwinkle-blue Vengold silk. "That's exactly why I chose to wear it for tonight's betrothal ceremony. I've got very fond memories of it, too—extremely fond memories."

"And what was I wearing?" he asked playfully.

"You were naked, of course," she answered as she went to him. He wrapped his arms around her and kissed the back of her neck, just as he had in the first vision. Tiny shivers ran up and down her spine. "Well, you were naked in all of them."

"Of course I was."

In their reflection, with him behind her, his hair fell in dark waves, the ocean blue of his eyes sparkled, and a slow, crooked smile spread across his face. "I've got to be the luckiest man alive, Neyla. I had stopped dreaming of a future, until I met you. You gave me hope again. You gave me a life."

She reached back and caressed his jaw. "I feel exactly the same about you." And she'd said as much in front of Saffira, the *taghta* magistrate, during the court proceedings last week.

He slipped out of his robe and slid his large hands up her arms, careful not to touch where she'd picked out the microchip with a heated needle.

"You know, you don't have to do it manually," she told his mirrored reflection. "You can use your Talent to undress me."

"I rather like the old-fashioned way. I want to savor this moment and sear it into my mind so that I never forget."

He opened the clasp and the gown slipped off her shoulders. Unlike the first time he'd undressed her, this time he wasn't going anywhere. She kept her gaze glued to the mirror and watched as he nuzzled her neck and caressed her breasts. She resisted the urge to turn in his arms—she hadn't done so in her vision.

"I rather miss these images," she said as his hand slid over her belly. "Why do you suppose we no longer see them?"

"It was destiny. We were meant to find each other and fall in love. At least, that's what Rosamund believes."

She caught his eye in the mirror. "You told Rosamund about our sex visions?"

He laughed. "Just that you seduced me and I fell for you."

"You have a very selective memory. I seem to remember just the opposite. What else did Rosamund say?"

"When we were traveling along different pathways keeping us apart, those visions were meant to remind us what our future together would hold. Once we started to draw closer and fall in love, our destiny became more concrete and those visions were no longer necessary."

"You mean, they were like a gentle nudge, a riding crop to correct us and get us heading in the right direction."

"Little soldier," he said, his eyes twinkling with mischief, "you surprise me."

"I do? Why?"

"I had no idea you'd be up for a little spanking."

"Oh, you'd be surprised, assassin. I'm very adventurous. I explored a new world to find you."

She melted into him as he carried her to the bed.

Pressing her lips to the yellowed bruising on his chest where one of the bullets had bounced from his skin, she pulled him on top of her.

She held her breath, waiting for that delicious sensation when his thick velvety tip would find her center and push inside. Instead, he kissed his way down her belly and nestled himself between her legs.

She trembled in anticipation of what he was about to do. His dark hair tickled her inner thighs, his breath hot on her sex. Like the dominant male who knew his partner well, he didn't ask if he could do this to her. He just expected that she would want the same thing he did.

"You are so beautiful," he said, spreading her knees wider.

She moaned when his mouth came down over her. As his tongue stroked her inside, her hips moved in the same synchronized rhythm. It took only a moment until she was gripped by a powerful orgasm. She clutched at his hair as wave after wave of pleasure coursed through her.

When the intensity began to fade, she was left with a warm, satisfied glow. She opened her eyes to find that he was staring at her, a smile creasing his face.

"What?"

"Are you always this easy to please, little soldier?"

Her cheeks heated. "I…uh…"

"I barely put my mouth on you before you took your

pleasure."

Took my pleasure? She loved his strange turns of phrase. "What can I say? I'm easy because you totally turn me on." She tugged on his shoulders. "Come up here now. I need to feel you inside me."

"This wasn't enough?" he chuckled. "I thought you'd like that instead."

"Instead? I want both." Despite her efforts, he climbed up and lay next to her. That was when she noticed tiny lines of worry crinkling the corners of his eyes. "Is something wrong?"

He had a faraway look again. "This setting, this bed, your hair as it's splayed out over the pillows like this—it's all from my first dream."

"Yes, and...?"

"If we make love right now, I believe my seed will start a baby growing in your belly. At least, if my vision was correct, it will."

Her heart stuttered a moment before it felt as if it would pop from her chest. A baby? Rickert's visions were of starting a family? She supposed the army birth control shot had worn off by now.

Once she joined START, the dreams she'd had of one day becoming a mother had quickly faded away. With her unpredictable schedule and the army basically owning her, she couldn't imagine juggling the needs of an infant, too. So that's what he'd seen through the mist?

Wow. She hadn't been expecting that. Her visions had only been about mind-blowing sex. Did that make her the shallower of the two?

"It'll take me awhile to destroy the portal with just a pickaxe," he said. "Perhaps we should wait till we're more settled somewhere else."

"Petra told me that the old monks are predicting more secret portals will be opening up soon. I can't stomach the thought of waiting for Pacificans to find them and come looking for more children."

"But Neyla, you heard Saffira at the proceedings. After this portal is destroyed, I am to be banished from Crestenfahl."

"You're still a Warrior of the Iron Guild. Can't we talk Lord Tierney out of it? Saffira said her judgment was merely an opinion, that he had the final decision. If it hadn't been for you, people would have suffered, and who knows how many babies taken."

She shuddered as she thought about Petra's newborn son. She'd been honored to witness his birth just a few days ago. Petra had named him Fallon, in honor of her brother.

Rickert ran a hand through his thick, raven hair and sighed. Had the locket been on his wrist, she had no doubt he'd have been fidgeting with it too, but he hadn't worn it since they day they'd defeated Gravich and his men.

"If it weren't for me," he said, "none of this would've happened in the first place. I lied to my people and I lied to a man I deeply respect. No, I will not ask Lord Tierney for a lighter sentence. I will take the punishment I deserve."

She cupped his chin, forcing him to look at her. This man she loved was iron strong and had such an honorable heart. Surely there had to be another solution.

"I'm not going to let you shoulder all of this, Rickert. I'm to blame as well." She paused, thinking. "What if we move to the other side in order to expose what the army is doing? The average person over there has no idea."

"And you think they'll believe us? According to them, I'm a *barbarian*, Neyla. And you are too, now, because you'll soon be my wife."

Wife. She liked the sound of that, but she wouldn't let herself get sidetracked. "Some will believe us."

"The army would track you down, and who knows what they would do when they found you. No. I will not allow it."

She was not deterred. "I can protect us."

"Damn it, Neyla," he said, his eyes flashing. "I don't care about your Talent. I won't knowingly let you put yourself in danger like that. Just because Smythe and Gravich are gone, doesn't mean there aren't a host of others just like them to take their places."

"But—"

"Being a Protection-Talent can't prevent them from throwing you in jail," he growled.

Okay, she could see his point. She stared up at the tapestry-covered ceiling and thought about the first time she'd seen him in that cold, dark cave on the side of the mountain, wearing nothing but a leather kilt, boots, and a few weapons. "What if we set up a refuge on the other side for Cascadian warriors crossing through the new portals?"

Rickert frowned. "A refuge?"

"A safe house. A compound. Whatever you want to call it. Your men need clothing and a place to stay while they're battling the raiders from Pacifica. It can be an operations base of sorts. You can lead them from the other side."

He blew out a long breath. "I don't know, Neyla."

"It's much better than the system you have in place now. Asher told me about stealing clothes and fashioning your own, as well as those makeshift campsites. When you can't cross through with any items, at least there could be a place on the other side where you can get those things. Regroup. Strategize. Rest."

He paused a moment, deep in thought, before he finally spoke. "You will not be able to enter your old life, Neyla."

"As if I would want to be in the army again," she said sarcastically.

"I'm not talking about the army. I'm talking about living in New Seattle. It's too dangerous."

"We don't have to live in the city. I'm a country girl at heart, anyway. Horses. Remember?" She could tell he was caving when he didn't immediately respond, so she forged ahead. "There are good people over there. People who would be just as horrified as I was that this is going on and want to help. I doubt my mother knows the whole story. And my brother...well, for all I know, he's a foundling, too."

He smiled finally. "I fell in love with an amazing woman."

"So you'll speak to Lord Tierney?"

"Yes, I'll speak to him."

"And the Iron Guild?"

"As long as this safehouse idea furthers our goal to keep the enemy out of Cascadia, I am sure the Guild will be on board."

It felt as if a huge weight had been lifted from her shoulders. She couldn't bear the thought that Rickert wouldn't continue his life's work, fighting against those who had done such terrible things to his...*their*...people. "Good. Now, make love to me. You've made me wait long enough."

"But my vision..."

She silenced him with a kiss. "Listen, Rickert. I want to give you children, to make you a father, and I'm ready now if it happens. Since these images were what brought us together..." She let the words hang in the air. "But if you think it's best to wait, I'm fine with that, too."

For several long minutes, he ran a finger along the bottom side of her breast as if it helped clarify his thoughts. All it did for her was heat up her insides and make her want him even more. When he finally lifted his chin, his eyes were glittering with moisture.

"In that first vision, before I knew it was me, I thought about how lucky that man was. And when I knew they were creating a child from the lovemaking I'd just witnessed, I felt an aching so deep in my bones that it hurt, because I believed it was something I'd never know."

A lump formed in her throat. "You ache for a family?"

"Yes," he said softly, "but only when you are ready, lass."

"I am ready, Rickert, whether it happens tonight, next year, or ten years from now. Let's experience the beautiful vision you saw, and we'll see if it comes true."

He smiled and kissed her then, all traces of worry gone. "Praise the Fates, little soldier. I love you." Angling himself on top of her, he quickly pushed inside, filling her body, her mind, her soul.

This man, this utterly amazing man, was hers. Forever.

THE END

Be sure to look for the second book in the Iron Portal series, ROGUE'S PASSION, Asher's story, available now.

BOOKS BY LAURIE LONDON

Iron Portal Series

ASSASSIN'S TOUCH
ROGUE'S PASSION
WARRIOR'S HEART

Sweetblood Series
(*Dark, sexy vampires*)

BONDED BY BLOOD
EMBRACED BY BLOOD
TEMPTED BY BLOOD
SEDUCED BY BLOOD

E-novella
HIDDEN BY BLOOD

Anthologies
A VAMPIRE FOR CHRISTMAS
(*with Michele Hauf, Caridad Pineiro and Alexis Morgan*)

Laurie London is the New York Times and USA Today bestselling author of the Sweetblood and Iron Portal series—dark, sexy paranormal romance, set primarily in the Pacific Northwest. She lives on a small farm outside of Seattle with her husband, two children and a variety of animals.

www.LaurieLondonBooks.com

Made in the USA
San Bernardino, CA
19 July 2020

75444870R00102